How the Children Became Stars

How the Children Became Stars

*a family treasury of stories, prayers, and blessings
from around the world*

Aaron Zerah

SORIN BOOKS   Notre Dame, Indiana

To my daughter, Sari, and all children of spirit.
May you shine like the brightness of the heavens and
like the stars forever.

International Standard Book Number: 1-893732-17-7

Library of Congress Catalog Card Number: 00-102079

Cover and text design by Brian C. Conley

Printed and bound in the United States of America.

Contents

Introduction

All children love stories. We parents love them as well, because they connect us to our own souls by connecting us to the time-tested wisdom of all the world's peoples.

How the Children Became Stars brings together the great storytellers who over the centuries have passed on the wisdom of their people by telling stories to their children. Here you will find the whole world of spirit, from the Aboriginal hero who chased a kangaroo and discovered the sunrise, to the Zoroastrian "Noah" who helped save Creation from the death of winter. Angels, gods and goddesses, and all kinds of animals—greedy monkeys, magic fish, terrible lions, beautiful butterflies, and laughable coyotes—live in these extraordinary tales. The great teachers who have taught the ways of the spirit—Jesus, King Solomon, Muhammad, Krishna, Buddha, and many others who have taken the path to holiness—also live here.

How the Children Became Stars is composed of fifty-two sections, each speaking to a special spiritual theme for a given week and containing four elements:

1) a story;
2) "Bringing It Home," a "To Do" list—questions and activities to move the family through the week;
3) a daily blessing for a meal;
4) a daily prayer.

You and your family may begin your journey with Week One at any time of the year. Families have a tremendous variety of schedules and ways of meeting. Choose the times and settings that work best for you as you make *How the Children Became Stars* a regular part of family life.

And a note of encouragement: *How the Children Became Stars* is meant for all of us. The stories are written so that very young children may understand them, and even the youngest child may enjoy the telling. "Bringing It Home" activities require only an enthusiastic heart. The prayers and meal blessings are short and simple.

How the Children Became Stars is meant to be shared. As the spirit moves you, invite grandparents and other extended family members to join you. As the spirit moves you, invite friends, neighbors, and families of different faiths to join you and enlarge your family's spiritual circle.

May you and your family be blessed.

Rev. Aaron Zerah

How Turtle Helped Make the Earth
—TRADITIONAL NATIVE AMERICAN STORY

In the beginning, everything was dark. There was no sun, no moon, no stars in the sky. There was water everywhere and it was running very fast.

Two creatures came from the north on a small boat—Turtle and his friend. A rope made with feathers came down from the sky and, climbing down the rope, came Begins-the-Earth. He went right over to the boat and stepped in. His face was covered and could not be seen, but his body was bright like the sun.

Turtle asked, "Brother, can you make some dry land for me, so I can come out of the water sometimes?"

Begins-the-Earth turned to Turtle and said, "You want dry land; where am I going to get earth to make dry land?"

Turtle spoke up. "Tie a rock to my left arm. Then I'll dive down to the bottom of the water and get some." Turtle jumped into the deep water.

Turtle was down at the bottom of the water for six years. When Turtle finally came to the surface, all the earth he had gathered had been washed away by the water. He had just a little bit left under his nails.

Begins-the-Earth took a stone knife and scraped this little bit of earth from under Turtle's nails. Then he put it in his hand and rolled it into a ball the size of a pebble. Begins-the-Earth kept looking at the pebble. Four times he looked at it and in that time the ball had grown to be as big as the world.

The earth was now dry land and there were big mountains all around. That is how Turtle dove into the water and helped make the earth.

Bringing It Home

To Do This Week

❑ Together go outside and touch the earth. Each person in the family scoop up a handful of earth. Put all the earth together in one bowl or flower pot. Each person plant a quick-growing seed (wheat or alfalfa are excellent) in this earth.

❑ Each day, water the seeds as you say the blessing for this week. (Keep watering until the seeds have sprouted.)

❑ What Turtle did was hard and very courageous. Think about one thing each of you does every day that makes you like Turtle and tell each other.

❑ Turtle helped make the earth. You do something extra today to help the family.

❑ Together, bring your earth and seedlings to a neighbor or a friend.

12

Blessing for Meals of the Week

Praised be you, my Lord, for our Sister Mother Earth, who feeds us and keeps us and makes so many kinds of fruit.

—SAINT FRANCIS OF ASSISI

Prayer for the Week

Deep peace
of the running wave to you,
Deep peace
of the quiet earth to you.
Deep peace
of the air to you,
Deep peace
of the shining star to you.

— CELTIC CHRISTIAN PRAYER CHANT

Week 2

A Big Piece of the Sky

—TRADITIONAL AFRICAN STORY

There was a time when people did not have to plant seeds and harvest food to eat. The children did not have to carry water or wood for the cook-fires. When people got hungry they just reached up to the sky, broke off a piece, and ate it. The sky tasted very good.

The king of this land was called the Oba and he and all his people celebrated many festivals with drumming, dancing, and eating. But the sky was starting to get angry because people took far more than they could eat. They threw the leftover sky into big heaps of garbage.

One morning the sky, instead of shining brightly, became dark. Great clouds covered the Oba's palace and the sky called out, "Oba! I am warning you. If your people keep wasting my gifts, the sky will not be there for them to eat anymore." Oba was very afraid and he sent messengers to tell everyone. All the people—the children, too—were warned to eat the sky only when they were hungry.

And for a long while that is what they did. Then came the time of the great festival. The best dancers, even the Oba himself, danced and celebrated for many days. The Oba watched so that nobody took more than they could eat.

But on the very last night of the festival a woman named Adese and her husband Otolo came to the Oba's to celebrate. Adese was the kind of person who always wanted more. She wore so many heavy coral necklaces she could hardly walk. Still, she wished to get more of them. And Adese really loved to eat.

Adese had a great time at the Oba's palace and went home with Otolo. "How wonderful it was!" she thought, "The drumming and dancing, the beautiful clothes, and especially the food were all wonderful." Remembering how delicious the sky had tasted, Adese had to have more. She reached up and took a huge piece of sky. But it was so big, and Adese was already so full, she could only finish part of it. She just could not swallow one more bite.

"What have I done?" Adese shouted. "Otolo, come here. I must not throw away any of the sky. You eat it." Otolo tried, but he was too full. All the children were called but they had been to a party and were too stuffed to take more than a few very small bites.

The neighbors and all the villagers came, but Adese was still left with a big piece of sky on her hands. Finally she said, "What does one more piece matter anyway?" She threw it on the garbage heap and buried the heap out of sight behind her house.

Suddenly there was a great sound of thunder that shook the earth. Lightning flashed above the Oba's palace but no rain fell. "Oba! Mighty One!" the sky called with a great loud voice. "Your people have not been respectful. Now I am leaving and going far away."

"What will we eat? How will the people live?" the Oba cried out.

"All of you must learn to work the land and hunt for food," the sky answered. "Maybe then you will learn not to waste the gifts offered to you."

And from that day on all the people worked to have food to eat and the sky was far, far away just as it is today.

Bringing It Home

To Do This Week

☐ Imagine you're the sky. Is there anything you're angry about that someone in your family is wasting?

☐ Pretend you're Adese. Is there anything you're taking too much of?

☐ Ask yourself, "What is my favorite thing to eat or drink?" Today don't have any of your favorite food.

☐ If you see any garbage on the street or on the ground anywhere today, stop to pick it up and throw it out in a proper place.

☐ Go through your stuff. Find one thing that you don't use or of which you have extra and give it away to someone else.

☐ Parents: skip one meal today. Kids: Have one meal that is smaller than usual. Add up the money that the food you didn't eat would have cost and give that exact amount to a hunger organization.

Blessing for Meals of the Week

May we prepare and eat this food not for our own selfish satisfaction.
May we be nourished by this food and may we be of service to others.

—INSPIRED BY THE TRADITIONAL INDIAN HOLY BOOK,
THE BHAGAVAD GITA

Prayer for the Week

My lord of heaven and earth is full of blessing.
In his left hand he holds dancing plumes.
With his right he calls me to dance with him.
Oh, what sweet joy!

—TRADITIONAL CHINESE TEACHING

Week 3

How the Birds Became Friends
—TRADITIONAL BUDDHIST STORY

When the birds first flew in the sky, they were not friends. One bird would say to another, "I am better than you," and soon they would start to shout and fight.

But one day, the Pheasant met the Crow and just didn't feel like arguing. So, instead of picking a fight, the Pheasant said, "Crow, you are better than me."

The Crow was very surprised and very happy to hear what the Pheasant said. So, to be polite, he answered, "No, Pheasant. You are a better bird than I am."

And they sat down together on a tree branch and began to talk. After a while, the Pheasant said, "Crow, I like being with you."

"I like you too, Pheasant," the Crow said.

They decided to live together in a big tree.

The longer they stayed together, the more the two birds liked each other, and the more they treated each other with kindness.

All the other birds saw how the Pheasant and the Crow stayed together and didn't yell or fight. Finally, some of the birds decided to see if the Pheasant and Crow really were friends. When the Crow was away, they came and asked the Pheasant, "Why do you stay with that awful crow?"

"You shouldn't say such things," the Pheasant told them. "The Crow is a better bird than I am and he kindly lets me live with him in this tree."

The next day the Pheasant was away and the troublesome birds came to see the Crow. "Crow," they asked him, "why do you stay with that awful Pheasant?"

"Please don't say that," said the Crow. "The Pheasant is a better bird than I am and he kindly lets me live with him in this tree."

The birds saw that the Pheasant and the Crow really did care about each other. They said to themselves, "Instead of fighting, why can't we be like the Pheasant and the Crow?"

And from then on, all the birds knew how to become friends.

Bringing It Home

To Do This Week

❏ Is there someone (or some animal) you just don't like? Write that person or animal's name on a piece of paper. Write or draw what you think you don't like about that person or animal. On that same piece of paper, write or draw one thing you do like about that person or animal. Make it really big.

❏ Still on that same paper, write one bad thing you have thought about that person or animal. If you have said something bad about them or hurt them, write that down, too.

❏ Say this prayer silently or out loud: "May my friend [the person or animal's name] be at peace."

❏ Say this prayer silently or out loud: "May I [your name] be at peace."

❏ As a family, share your papers and tell your stories.

Blessing for Meals of the Week

*Blessed are You, our God, Holiest One of the Universe,
who creates all the living beings, for all the things
You have created to sustain every living being.*

—TRADITIONAL JEWISH BLESSING

Prayer for the Week

*We love God for
God teaches the birds
To sing lovely songs.
We love God for
God loves children and
Blesses them with intelligence and goodness.*

—INSPIRED BY A TRADITIONAL HINDU PRAYER

Who's to Blame?

— TRADITIONAL TAOIST CHINESE STORY

One day, a woodcutter went out to chop a load of firewood to sell in the market, but his favorite ax was gone. He looked all through the wood-pile, behind his house, and even in his house. He looked everywhere he thought he might have put the ax, but he did not find it. The more he looked, the more upset and frustrated he became. He exhausted himself looking for his precious ax.

Then he noticed a boy—his neighbor's son—standing near the wood-shed. The woodcutter stared at the boy and thought to himself: "What's he doing hanging around the woodshed, just walking back and forth? He's got his hands behind his back and his face has a guilty look. Why that boy must have stolen my ax! I can't prove it, but I'll make that boy pay anyhow."

The next day the woodcutter walked over to a pile of firewood he had forgotten about and tripped on something. It was his ax! "Oh yes," he remembered, "that's where I left it when I was cutting wood the other day."

Then the woodcutter saw the neighbor's son again. He inspected the boy up and down, from head to toe. He looked at him right in the eye. "How strange," the woodcutter thought, "today the boy looks completely innocent."

Bringing It Home

To Do This Week

❏ Imagine you are the woodcutter. What would you do differently? Imagine you are the boy. What would you do differently than the boy did?

❏ Tell a story about when you were accused of something you didn't do.

❏ Tell a story about when you thought someone did something they really didn't do.

❏ Pick one person in your family and apologize for blaming him or her for something they didn't do.

❏ Is there something you've done about which you feel guilty? Talk about it.

Blessing for Meals of the Week

We are happy, dear Lord
because you have accepted us in your heart.
We swim in your grace
like a whale in the ocean.
This food you give us
shows us your grace.

—INSPIRED BY A TRADITIONAL AFRICAN PRAYER

Prayer for the Week

May the blessing of God rest upon you,
May his peace abide with you,
May his presence light up your heart,
Now and forevermore.

—TRADITIONAL SUFI BLESSING

Week 5

Gluscabi's Magic Bag and the Animals

— TRADITIONAL NATIVE AMERICAN STORY

When he was young, Gluscabi went hunting in the forest for some animals to eat. He was hungry.

But even though Gluscabi walked very quietly in his moccasins, the animals sensed he was there and hid from him. Gluscabi did not catch a single one. He returned home and sat down near his Grandmother Woodchuck's wigwam.

"Hunting is too hard," Gluscabi said, and he began to sing a wishing song for a game bag to make hunting easier. Grandmother heard his singing and she made him a special game bag with hair from a deer, but Gluscabi was not satisfied with it. Then Grandmother wove moose hairs into the bag, but Gluscabi kept on singing. Finally Grandmother took some hair from her own belly and sewed it into the bag. Now the bag could stretch and stretch, and become bigger and bigger.

Gluscabi was pleased with this magic game bag and carried it back to the forest with him. He called out, "All animals, listen to my warning. The earth is going to be destroyed. I have come to help you."

The animals were scared but eventually they crept toward Gluscabi and asked how he meant to help them. Gluscabi held out the magic bag and said, "Climb in here and you will not see the end of the world."

One by one the rabbits, muskrats, porcupines, deer, squirrels, raccoons, and bears—all the animals of the forest—climbed into Gluscabi's open bag. Gluscabi tied the bag closed with all the animals in it and ran home. He was very happy. "I never have to go hunting again," he said to himself.

But soon Grandmother asked Gluscabi, "What's making all that noise?"

Gluscabi showed her the magic bag. "See," he said, "I'm so smart. I got all the animals to go into the bag. Now whenever we want to eat meat we can take one out."

Grandmother was not pleased. "Listen, Gluscabi," she said, "the forest is quiet. There are no animals left in the forest, and all the animals in your bag will die without food and water. They cannot breathe. There will be no animals left in the world." Grandmother looked at Gluscabi and asked, "Is this the gift you are leaving to the world?"

Gluscabi said to Grandmother, "No. I want my children, their children, and all their children to live with the animals. I did this because hunting is so hard."

Grandmother said, "Hard work will make you strong and smart. The animals will become wiser too when you hunt them. Some will always get away from the arrows you shoot and the traps you set. All will live in balance. This is a good way."

Gluscabi agreed. He took the magic bag back to the forest and let all the animals go. He shouted, "The danger has passed. You are safe now." And all the animals went back to their place in the forest. Gluscabi listened to Grandmother, so we still see animals everywhere on the earth.

Bringing It Home

To Do This Week

❏ What things do you not like to do because they are hard for you?
Write down three of them. Choose one of the three things and do it
today. Do it better or longer than you usually do.

❏ Draw a picture of how you felt after the work you did above.

❏ Imagine you are Gluscabi and you've just let all the animals go.
What do you do now? Imagine you are one of the animals, now back
in your forest home. What will you do to stay alive? Discuss this
with your family.

Blessing for Meals of the Week

You, O Tsui-Goab!
Lord, father of our fathers,
Let our animals live!
Let us also live,
That we may bless you!
You, father of the fathers!
You, our Lord!
You, O Tsui-Goab!

—TRADITIONAL AFRICAN PRAYER

Prayer for the Week

O God, we have devoted our hearts to you,
For we have no other safe place in the world.
Give us the strength we need.
Let us be ambitious and willing to work every day.
Let us please our mothers and our fathers.
May our hard work bring prosperity to our land.
Amen.

—INSPIRED BY A TRADITIONAL IRANIAN PRAYER

Week 6

How Kindness Leads to Great Joy
—TRADITIONAL BUDDHIST STORY

In the land of Gandhara in India, there lived a Brahmin, a good and noble man. He was given a young ox-calf as a present and was so happy with the ox that he named him Great Joy.

He treated the young ox with kindness, feeding him rice and other special foods. Great Joy grew and grew, until he was very, very big and very, very strong.

One day Great Joy said to himself, "The Brahmin has been so loving and kind to me and I have grown to be the strongest, most powerful bull in all the land. Now I want to do something for him."

So Great Joy walked over to the Brahmin's house and said, "Kind sir, I know a way I can repay you for your goodness to me. Please listen." Great Joy told the Brahmin to go to town and say to the merchants there: "My ox, Great Joy, is so strong that he can pull a hundred carts filled with sand, gravel, and stones." When a rich merchant answered, "That is impossible," the Brahmin was to say, "I will bet you one thousand pieces of silver he can do it!"

The Brahmin went to town, found a merchant, and made the bet for one thousand pieces of silver. They agreed that the next day Great Joy would try to pull the hundred carts, all filled with sand and rocks. The whole town turned out to see what would happen. Could a single ox pull such a heavy load?

The Brahmin harnessed Great Joy to the line of carts and then climbed into a seat right behind him. He gave the ox some grain to eat and then, waving his driving stick, the Brahmin shouted at the top of his voice, "Now, you beast, you devil, pull with all your strength!" And then the Brahmin hit the ox with the stick.

"Beast? Devil? What is it that you call me?" Great Joy thought, and he refused to move. The Brahmin cursed and threatened him more, but Great Joy stood his ground. Everybody laughed and hollered and made fun of the Brahmin and his ox. Finally the Brahmin had to release Great Joy, pay the merchant one thousand pieces of silver and go home.

The Brahmin was heartbroken and, crying many tears, he went to bed. Great Joy went to the window, peeked in, and asked the Brahmin, "Why are you crying, my friend?"

"How can you ask this question?" the Brahmin wailed. "You know I have lost all my money today. Everyone in the town is laughing at me, and it's all because of you."

"Dear Brahmin," said the ox, "in all my days living with you, have I ever tramped through your garden? Or broken a plow? Or stepped on your children's feet?"

"No," answered the Brahmin. "In truth, you have never done any harm to me."

"Then why did you call me names like 'beast' and 'devil' today, and hit me with your stick?" Great Joy asked. "Do I not deserve to be treated with kindness?"

The Brahmin, hearing this, was ashamed. He knew the ox was right. In kindness, Great Joy said, "Look. Let us start over again. Go back to the merchant and bet him two thousand pieces of silver. Be kind to me and we will win!"

The Brahmin followed Great Joy's advice and the bet was made. Again the carts were loaded, the townspeople came to watch, and Great Joy readied himself to pull. This time, the Brahmin held the stick in his hand and gently said, "My good friend, my dear brother, my Great Joy, you have the strength. Please pull the carts now."

And with one great pull, Great Joy pulled the carts. At first they moved just a little. Then the carts got rolling and Great Joy pulled them all the way out of town and back again.

The Brahmin was paid the two thousand pieces of silver and everyone cheered for Great Joy.

Bringing It Home

To Do This Week

❑ Imagine you are the ox, Great Joy. What would you have done when the Brahmin yelled at you?

❑ Are there people in your family you have made fun of or laughed at? Tell them you are sorry. Has someone in your family been especially good to you? Say thank you and give each one a hug.

❑ Do something kind today for an animal.

❑ Today give three friends, sisters, or brothers words of encouragement. Tell them you know they can accomplish whatever they want. Ask someone in your family to tell you how strong you are and that you will succeed in what you do.

❑ Write or draw what it feels like when you are kind to someone and when someone is kind to you.

Blessing for Meals of the Week

This food comes from the Earth and the Sky.
It is the gift of the whole universe
And the fruit of much strong work:
May we live in a way that makes us worthy to receive it.

—TRADITIONAL BUDDHIST BLESSING

Prayer for the Week

Hear, O Israel,
the Lord Our God, the Lord is One.
And you shall love the Lord your God
with all your heart, with all your soul, with all your strength.
And these words which I command to you this day
shall be upon your heart.
And you shall teach them to your children
and shall talk of them when you sit in your house,
and when you walk by the way,
and when you lie down,
and when you rise.

—FROM HEBREW SCRIPTURES

Week 7

A Very Good Story
—TRADITIONAL JEWISH STORY

When Israel ben Eliezer was a very young boy in Poland, his parents died. The people in his village took care of him and made him go to school to study the Torah, the Jewish holy books.

But young Israel had very little desire to stay inside the school room and study. He wanted to wander in the forest just beyond the village. When he was with the trees and the animals and all the beautiful things of nature, Israel felt God was there with him.

When he became a man, Israel helped many sick people to get well and many uneducated people to understand how God wanted them to have a good and happy life. He was called the Baal Shem Tov, the Master of the Good Name, because he knew how to talk to God.

The Baal Shem Tov shared the story of his childhood walks in the forest and how he prayed there with his friends. This is a story they told to their friends, who told it to others, and so on to today.

The Baal Shem Tov (Master of the Good Name), may he be remembered, used to go to a certain place in the forest whenever he faced an especially difficult situation. There he would light a fire and pray, and whatever needed to be done was done.

After the Baal Shem Tov died, his successor followed in his footsteps, and he, too, went to the very same place in the forest. He said, "We cannot light the fire anymore, for we don't know the Master's way with it, but we can say the prayer." And whatever he asked in prayer was, as before, done.

This generation passed, and the pious Rabbi Moshe Lieb went to the woods and said, "The fire we are unable to light, and the prayer is gone from our minds. All we know is this holy place in the forest, and that will have to do." His prayers also came to be.

In the fourth generation, Rabbi Israel of Rishen no longer made the journey to the holy place. He stayed at home, for, as he said, "The fire we cannot light, the prayer we don't know anymore, nor do we remember the right place to go. All we can do is tell the story."

And that, too, was quite enough.

Bringing It Home

To Do This Week

- ❏ The boy Israel liked to walk in the forest. Take a walk wherever you want. Write on a special paper three things that you really paid attention to during your walk.

- ❏ Imagine you are eighteen years older than you are now. Write down on the paper three things you see yourself doing.

- ❏ Write down on the paper three things you want to do for (a) yourself, (b) your family, (c) the world. Then, write three things you are praying for (a) yourself, (b) your family, (c) the world.

- ❏ Now, create a story about you and your life and write it on the other side of the paper. The Baal Shem Tov loved to tell stories to his friends because he knew they enjoyed them so much. Be like the Baal Shem Tov. Tell your story.

Blessing for Meals of the Week

Let the grass grow around me
Let the wind move in near silence
And the sun give sustenance to its creation

—PRAYER OF REV. AARON ZERAH

Prayer for the Week

Grant me the ability to be alone;
may it be my way every day to go outdoors
among the trees and grasses,
among all growing things,
and there may I be alone,
to talk with the one
that I belong to.

—PRAYER OF RABBI NACHMAN OF BRATZLAV

Week 8

Gideon Becomes a Hero

— TRADITIONAL STORY FROM HEBREW SCRIPTURES

Young Gideon lived in Israel during a terrible time. Whenever the grapes or grain were ready to be harvested, hordes of enemies riding swiftly on camels came out of the desert to steal the crops. They took sheep, goats, and cattle, too.

Nothing and nobody was safe. Gideon and the people did their best to hide their food—and themselves—but after seven years of such raids, they had almost nothing left. The Israelites, who had forgotten to do what God taught them, prayed to God for help.

One day Gideon was hiding wheat from the desert people when an angel appeared under an oak tree right near him and said, "Gideon, God is with you, you mighty man of courage. Go and save your people."

And Gideon said to the angel, "How can I be the one to save Israel?"

The angel of God answered, "God will be with you and you will defeat your enemies—thousands though they may be—as if they were only one man."

Then the enemies of the Israelites gathered themselves together in a great army. They were a terrifying sight to see as they prepared to attack. Gideon blew a horn calling to the tribes of Israel to come together and get ready to fight.

But Gideon was not sure he really could be a hero and that God was with him. He said to God, "If you will save Israel by my hand as you have promised, then I ask for a sign. I will put a piece of wool on the ground. Tomorrow if there is dew on the wool but the ground is dry, I will know you are truly with me." And it was so. The wool was soaking wet with dew, but the ground was dry.

Still, Gideon was afraid. He said to God: "Prove it to me once more. This time make the earth wet with dew but the wool dry." And God did make it so.

Gideon and many thousands of men then started off to battle, but God told Gideon that any who were afraid should stay back. Twenty-two thousand returned home. Ten thousand remained, and God said to Gideon, "You have too many soldiers."

God told Gideon that only three hundred should go with him to fight the much greater number of the enemy. When they won the victory, the Israelites would know that God was with them.

So Gideon, the young man who never thought he would be a hero, led his men to meet the enemy. Gideon again blew his horn, and this time so did Israelites on all sides of the enemy camp. Shouting "The sword of God, the sword of Gideon falls upon you!" they surprised the enemy soldiers, causing them to panic and attack each other. The enemy fled, and Gideon was the hero of all the people.

Bringing It Home

To Do This Week

Imagine you are Gideon. Draw or paint a picture of the angel who came to see you.

Remember a time when you were afraid someone would hurt you. What did you do? Is there someone you're afraid of now? Draw a picture of that person. Tell each other what scares you about that person. When one of you is talking about it, everyone else listens.

Pray that an angel, a messenger from God, will come to talk to you.

Share with each other what happened. Did you feel anything? Did you receive a message?

Look at the pictures you made of the angel and the person who scared you together. Now if you are sure what heroic action to take, go do it. If you are still not clear, pray for the angel to come again.

Blessing for Meals of the Week

From that treasure, O Lord,
Always with you where you live,
Give to us that we may live.

—INSPIRED BY A TRADITIONAL HINDU PRAYER

Prayer for the Week

I believe in the sun even when it is not shining.
I believe in love even when feeling it not.
I believe in God even when he is silent.

—TRADITIONAL JEWISH PRAYER

Week 9

The Monkeys Reach for the Moon
—TRADITIONAL BUDDHIST STORY

One night the king of the monkeys looked down from a high cliff to the water far below. He saw the brilliant silver moon reflected in the water and thought, "That is the most beautiful jewel I have ever seen. I must find a way to get it."

He told all the other monkeys about the beautiful jewel he had seen, hoping they would help him get it. But they all said, "It will be so difficult to get."

Then the king of the monkeys had an idea. "Look," he said, "here's how it can be done. One of you will climb a tall tree and hold on tight. Stick out your tail and the next monkey will hold onto it. Each monkey will hold onto the tail of the one above, making a long, long chain down to the water. Then the last monkey will be able to reach the jewel."

So the monkeys, five hundred of them, followed the king of the monkeys' plan and, one by one, they held on tight to the tail of the monkey above them. All of them were connected in the chain to the first monkey, who was holding tightly to the tree. Just as the last monkey was about to reach the object that the king of the monkeys so desired, the weight of the monkeys proved to be too much and the monkey holding onto the tree let go. All five hundred monkeys fell into the water and all five hundred monkeys drowned.

Bringing It Home

To Do This Week

❏ Write down one thing you really want. Draw or paint a picture of that thing.

❏ Share a story about when someone you know really wanted to get something and asked you to help. Share a story about when you really wanted something and you asked others to help you.

❏ Imagine you are one of the monkeys. What would you do when the king of the monkeys came up with his idea to make the chain?

❏ Imagine you are the king of the monkeys. Would you join the chain or stand back and watch?

❏ If you were a monkey from another place and you saw what happened, what would you tell your monkey friends when you got back home?

Blessing for Meals of the Week

Blessed by the Lord be the land,
With the precious gifts of heaven,
With the precious fruits brought forth by the sun
And the riches brought forth by the moon.

—FROM HEBREW SCRIPTURES

Prayer for the Week

Dear Mother,
Hear and bless
All the animals
And keep with tenderness
Small creatures.

—ADAPTED FROM A TRADITIONAL CHRISTIAN PRAYER

Week 10

The Two Foolish Cats

—TRADITIONAL JAPANESE STORY

In the hills of Japan a long while ago two cats lived together. One was black and very big and the other a tabby, much smaller in size. They were the best of friends, these two, and were very good to each other.

One day, each of them found a most delightful treat—a fresh, sweet rice cake. "Look at mine!" the big cat cried out. He held it in his paws and said, "It looks so delicious!"

The small cat said, "Well, look at my cake. It smells more wonderful than a fat field mouse!"

So the two cats sat down together to look at each other's cakes and compare them. They soon noticed that the two cakes were very different in size. The big cat had a small cake and the small cat a much bigger one.

"I'm big, so I should have the big cake," the black cat complained. "Let us swap." But the little tabby hissed and threatened to bite his friend. "I am small, so I need to eat the bigger one. I will never trade with you."

They started calling each other names, and soon they were snarling and trying to scratch each other. For hours the big cat and the small cat chased each other around the trees and howled.

Finally, the black cat, out of breath, said, "Let us stop this fighting. We cannot come to an agreement, but let us go see the wise monkey and let him make equal shares of the rice cakes for us."

As the cakes were already beginning to get hard, the small cat agreed. Both cats wanted to eat the cakes while they were still fresh and tasty, so they hurried off to find the wise monkey. Into the forest, through thick grasses and vines and over many fallen logs they ran, calling out, "Mr. Monkey! Mr. Monkey!"

At last there he was, sitting in a high branch of a tree, wearing a red hat. The wise monkey held a set of golden scales in his hands that he used to solve problems just like the one the two cats had.

They talked both at once but the wise monkey soon understood. "Oh, I see your difficulty," he said with a serious voice. "How right you were to come to me."

He promised that each cat would get an equal share. With that he took the two cakes from them and put one on each side of the scale. The sides did not balance because the big cake was much heavier than the small one. "Your quarrel was quite understandable," the wise monkey said. "The big piece is much heavier. I will have to take a bite to even them out." And he did.

But he took too much, and now the other cake was the heavier one. "Oh no," the wise monkey said. "Now I shall have to take another bite." So he did, but once again the two cakes were not equal. The wise monkey kept taking bites out of one and then the other and both cakes got smaller and smaller. The two cats cried out. "That's enough!" and, "They must be even now!" but the clever monkey paid no attention to them. He kept weighing and eating and weighing and eating until he had eaten up all of both rice cakes.

"Well," he said to the cats, "you see, both cakes are equal now. That is what you came for, is it not? There is nothing left for you to quarrel about."

And the two cats never did quarrel again.

Bringing It Home

To Do This Week

❏ Pretend you're the big cat. How do you feel when you first find the rice cake? Pretend you're the small cat. How do you feel when you first find the rice cake?

❏ How do you feel when you see someone has something better than what you have? Do you ask to share? How do you feel when you have something better than someone else? Do you offer to share?

❏ Tell a story about how you shared something without fighting. How did you feel afterwards?

❏ Pretend you are the monkey. What would you do when the two quarreling cats came to see you?

❏ Imagine you are the two cats. How do you feel at the end of the story?

Blessing for Meals of the Week

Blessed are you
O Lord our God,
King of the world,
Who brings forth bread from the earth.

—TRADITIONAL JEWISH BLESSING

Prayer for the Week

The one who gives away wealth
and does no favors for anyone to get a reward,
only seeking to please the Lord, the Most High;
This one shall surely be satisfied.

—FROM THE QUR'AN, HOLY BOOK OF ISLAM

Week 11

The Intelligent Donkey

—TRADITIONAL STORY FROM HEBREW SCRIPTURES

Balak, the King of Moab, looked upon the great multitude of the people of Israel. They surrounded his land and he was afraid of what they would do.

Balak sent messengers to bring back a man named Balaam, known to be able to see wisely into the future. He wanted Balaam to curse the people of Israel, for whomever Balaam blessed was blessed, and whomever he cursed was cursed. But God told Balaam he must not curse them. "They are blessed," God told Balaam.

"If Balak would give me his own house filled with silver and gold, still I will not speak against the word of God," Balaam told the messengers. He refused to go.

That night God visited Balaam again. He said, "Rise up to go with these men of Balak and listen to what I tell you to do."

Balaam saddled his donkey the next morning and started on his journey with the men of Moab. But God was angry that Balaam had chosen to go. He sent an angel with a sword to block his way.

The donkey saw the terrible angel and turned away from the road into a field. But Balaam, seeing nothing, beat the donkey to force the beast back onto the road. Soon the path led through a vineyard with high walls on either side. The angel again appeared to bar the way. Balaam's donkey saw the angel and, trying to escape, she crushed Balaam's foot against the wall. He again beat the donkey. Then the angel appeared once more, this time standing in the narrowest pathway. The donkey could go neither left nor right, so she simply fell down underneath Balaam on the road. Balaam grew even angrier, and he hit the donkey much harder than before.

Then God opened the donkey's mouth and she said, "What have I done to you that you have beaten me three times now?"

"Because you have played tricks with me," Balaam shouted. "Had I a sword with me, I would kill you!"

Then God opened Balaam's eyes. He saw the angel and instantly he fell flat on his face before him.

"Surely," the angel said to Balaam, "if it were not for your donkey I would have killed you and saved her. Go now to Moab and speak the word of God."

Three times Balak asked Balaam to curse the Israelites, but he did not. The last time Balaam stood on a high mountain and, seeing the good people gathered, he called out a great blessing.

"I called on you to curse them," Balak swore at the seer. "I would have made you rich; now you must go back with nothing in your hands."

So Balaam and the donkey returned to their home.

Bringing It Home

To Do This Week

❑ Have you said bad words or cursed someone you didn't like? What happened?

❑ Share a story about when someone did something, like the donkey did with Balaam, that you didn't want them to do.

❑ Imagine you are Balaam's donkey. Would you act differently after you were beaten by Balaam? Imagine you are the angel. Would you act differently after Balaam hit the donkey?

❑ Imagine you are Balaam and Balak keeps offering you more and more money and riches if you will speak a lie. What would you do?

❑ Imagine you are looking through the eyes of God. Whom in this story do you see as unwise and whom do you see as intelligent?

Blessing for Meals of the Week

O Great Spirit, now that I am about to eat,
Give my thanks to the beasts and birds
Whom you have provided for my hunger.
And I ask you to share my sadness that
The living creatures must die
For me to live and be well.

—TRADITIONAL NATIVE AMERICAN PRAYER

Prayer for the Week

The sin which I have done, turn into goodness.
The bad deeds which I have committed, let the wind carry away.
O God I know and God I do not know,
My bad deeds are seven times seven; take them from me;
O Goddess I know and Goddess I do not know,
My bad deeds are seven times seven; take them from me.
Take them from me and I will sing your praise.

—TRADITIONAL MESOPOTAMIAN PRAYER

A Jealous Family

—TRADITIONAL STORY FROM HEBREW SCRIPTURES

Israel was happy to be the father of such a large family. He had twelve sons and one daughter and, together with the children's mothers, they all lived in the land of Canaan.

But of all the children, Joseph, the next to last-born of the boys, was Israel's favorite. Joseph's mother, Rachel, was Israel's most beloved wife, and when she died giving birth to Joseph's younger brother Benjamin, Israel grieved greatly. Because he loved Rachel so much, Israel looked upon Joseph, her first-born son, as his own first-born.

Israel gave Joseph special gifts. One of the gifts was a many-colored coat, the kind that was only worn by the privileged son. Joseph's older brothers were very angry and jealous.

To make matters worse, Joseph had two powerful dreams. In each dream his brothers had become Joseph's servants. They became even angrier with him.

The brothers went out to take care of the family's flock of sheep a good distance away, but Joseph stayed home. After a while his father sent Joseph to find his brothers and report back if the brothers and the sheep were well.

When the brothers saw Joseph coming, all dressed up in his special coat, they angrily talked among themselves and said, "Let us kill him." But at last they decided to throw him into a pit instead. They tore off his coat and splashed sheep's blood on it and returned home. They told their father that they had found the coat and Joseph must have been eaten by a lion!

Meanwhile, Joseph was rescued by men who took him to Egypt as a slave. Eventually Joseph's dreams came true and he became the trusted advisor to the ruler of all Egypt. Joseph forgave his brothers and helped save the whole family from starvation. Then they all lived together again.

Bringing It Home

To Do This Week

❏ Write the name of one person in your family you are jealous of. Write down on the paper next to the first name the name of someone you think is jealous of you.

❏ Choose one person in your family with whom you spend the least time. Ask her or him to do something special with you.

❏ Share with each other something special you do or you have created. First let the children speak, and the parents listen. Then let the parents speak, and the children listen.

❏ Draw or paint a picture of a many-colored coat you'd like to receive as a gift. Give the picture to the one you are jealous of.

Blessing for Meals of the Week

Give us, Lord, a bit of sun,
a bit of work and a bit of fun;
give us all in the struggle and sputter
our daily bread and a bit of butter;
give us sense, for we're some of us duffers,
and a heart to feel for all that suffers.
Give us, Lord, a chance to be
our goodly best, brave, wise, and free;
our goodly best for ourself, and others,
'til all men learn to live as brothers.

—ADAPTED FROM A TRADITIONAL ENGLISH BLESSING

Prayer for the Week

What is my great offense, O god!
I have eaten standing perhaps, or
Without giving thanks,
Or these my people have eaten
Wrongfully.
Yes, that is the offense, O Kane-of-the-water-of-life.
O let me live, the one devoted to you
I call upon you
O god of my body who lives in the heavens.
O Kane, let the lightning flash, let the thunder roar,
Let the earth shake.
I am saved; my god has looked upon me and I am saved.
I am washed. I have escaped the danger.

—TRADITIONAL HAWAIIAN PRAYER

Week 13

False Friends

—TRADITIONAL GREEK FABLE OF AESOP

One day a fox fell into a very deep well. It was so deep that the fox, no matter how desperate, could not get out. The fox had just about given up hope when a goat came to the well to quench his thirst. He saw the fox and asked, "What are you doing in the well, old fox? Do you know if the water in this well is good to drink, my friend?"

The fox didn't let on that he was trapped in the well. Instead he told the goat peering over the edge of the well, "This is the finest water around. And you better jump right in and drink your fill now, because there's no rain coming for a long time. That's why I jumped in myself."

The goat got into the well as quickly as he could and, thanking the fox, drank all the water that he could. When he finished, the goat asked the fox, "How do we get out now?"

"Easy," said the fox. "You brace your strong legs against both walls of the well and lift your head up high. I'll climb up your back and push off the horns of your head and leap out of the well. When I'm out, I'll reach back down into the well and pull you out."

The goat agreed and the fox was out of the well in no time at all. Then the fox ran away and the goat was left stuck in the well.

Bringing It Home

To Do This Week

❏ Tell a story about how someone tricked you. Tell a story about how you tricked or wanted to trick someone else.

❏ Pretend you're the fox stuck in the well. What would you have said to the goat when he first saw you there? Pretend you're the goat. What would you have done when you first saw the fox in the well?

❏ Think about something with which you are having deep trouble, or a "well" in which you are stuck. Ask someone in your family for help. Ask someone in your family if there's some way they are stuck and need your help.

❏ Go to a neighbor's house together and ask if there is anything you can do to help them out.

Blessing for Meals of the Week

Blessed are the poor in spirit
for theirs is the kingdom of heaven.
Blessed are they who hunger and thirst after righteousness
for they shall be filled.

— FROM THE CHRISTIAN NEW TESTAMENT

Prayer for the Week

Lord, make me an instrument of your peace.
Where there is hatred, let me sow love,
Where there is injury, pardon,
Where there is doubt, faith,
Where there is despair, hope,
Where there is darkness, light,
Where there is sadness, joy.
O Divine Master, grant that I may not so much seek to be Consoled as to
console
Not so much to be understood as to understand
Not so much to be loved, as to love
For it is in giving that we receive
It is in pardoning that we are pardoned
It is in dying that we are born to eternal life.

—SAINT FRANCIS OF ASSISI

Bamapama's New Dream

—TRADITIONAL ABORIGINAL STORY OF AUSTRALIA

The original people of Australia tell the story of Bamapama, the crazy man. He lived in the Dreamtime where anything is possible.

Bamapama's people dwelled underground in a place where the sun stayed in one place all day long. It never went down and it was always very hot.

Bamapama decided one time to go up to the surface of the earth. "I'll go hunting," he said. When he got to the top he saw a big kangaroo. Bamapama started chasing it. But Bamapama couldn't get close enough to throw his spear, so as the kangaroo ran away to the west, Bamapama followed. The day was long and the sun was going down further and further in the sky. The kangaroo stopped running and Bamapama caught up to it. He was about to throw his spear when the sun fell completely below the horizon. It was now dark.

Bamapama had never seen night before. Where he lived it was always light. He became very frightened. Bamapama started to cry. He climbed a tree to see if he could find light high above, but it was dark there, too. So he climbed down the tree and fell asleep.

When he woke up the next day it was morning and the sky was light again. Bamapama was full of joy. Looking at the sun, he said, "Here they sleep at night and rise with the sun. This is a good way."

Bamapama went back home and everyone wanted to know where he had been. He told them all about chasing the kangaroo, the setting of the sun, and how when he woke up from the dark night, it was light in the sky once more. "Come and see," he said. "It's very different. You sleep at night and then the sun is up again. It is a good way to live."

He led all the people to the surface of the earth. The darkness came, the people were frightened, and like Bamapama, they, too, started climbing up trees. Bamapama said, "Don't be scared!" and the people came down and slept.

When the sun rose the next morning, the people stretched out in its warm rays. They said, "This is a good way to live. Much better than living under the earth where it is always so hot. And here if we get cold we can get wood from the trees and make a fire. This is a good place to stay."

So Bamapama and the people stayed above ground in the new place.

Bringing It Home

To Do This Week

❑ The next time you go outside, take a piece of paper with you. Write down three things you never noticed before and share what you saw with your family.

❑ Pretend you don't know anyone in your family at all. Tell them one thing you see about each of them.

❑ Move something important to you in your room to a different place or sleep in a different place than you usually do. Share how that felt.

❑ Think about some new place, school, or work you know you will go to in the future. Write or draw how you feel about going to that new place.

❑ Imagine you have never seen flowers in your life. Now for the first time you are about to see them. Draw or paint a picture of what you will see.

Blessing for Meals of the Week

*Thank you for the wind and rain
and sun and pleasant weather,
thank you for this our food
and that we are together.*

—CHRISTIAN MENNONITE BLESSING

Prayer for the Week

*O God you are my God; early will I seek you.
My soul thirsts for you, my body longs for you
In a dry and thirsty land.
Because your loving kindness is greater than life,
My mouth will sing praises of you.*

—FROM HEBREW SCRIPTURES

Week 15

Is It Fair?
—ADAPTED FROM THE CHRISTIAN NEW TESTAMENT

"Listen," Jesus told the people gathered around him, "and I will tell you about the kingdom of heaven.

"You see, the kingdom of heaven is like a man who went out at dawn to hire people to work in his vineyard. He agreed to pay them each a drachma as pay for a day's work. Then he sent them to work in the vineyard.

"A few hours later, he went out again, and seeing others standing about in the marketplace and not working, he said to them, 'You go to work in my vineyard, and I'll pay you a decent wage.' And they went, too. He went out again around noon and later in the afternoon and both times did the same thing.

"Very late in the afternoon he went out again and found still others standing around and said to them, 'Why are you not working, but just standing here?' They answered, 'Nobody came to hire us.' So he said, 'You go now to my vineyard and work.'

"When the day was gone, the owner of the vineyard called out to his manager and said, 'Gather together all the workers and pay them all, starting with the ones who got here last.' The ones who came very late in the day stepped forward and each received a drachma. When the first workers came forward, they expected they would get much more, but they each got a drachma, too.

"They started complaining to the vineyard owner, saying, 'Those last workers only worked an hour and you're paying them the same as us. We worked the whole day in the hot sun!'

"'But,' the owner responded to one of the complainers, 'I have not cheated you. We agreed on a drachma and that's what I gave you. Take the pay you are given and go your way. Am I not free to do as I wish with my own money? Are you envious because I am generous?'

"Thus," Jesus said, "the last will be first, and the first will be last."

Bringing It Home

To Do This Week

❏ Imagine you're in the first group of people. Are you happy when the vineyard owner offers you a chance to work? Imagine you're in the last group. How do you feel when the owner shows up and wants to hire you?

❏ Pretend you're the owner of the vineyard. What would you do when the first workers complained and wanted more money?

❏ Do you sometimes get less than someone else for doing the same kind of chore or work? Do you sometimes get more than someone else for doing the same kind of chore or work? How does it feel? Why do you think it happens?

❏ Why do you think Jesus told this story?

Blessing for Meals of the Week

*Today, today, today. Bless us God,
and help us to grow.*

—TRADITIONAL JEWISH PRAYER

Prayer for the Week

*O God, you are on high with the great spirits.
You lift up the grassy hills
Above the earth, and create the rivers,
O Gracious One.*

—TRADITIONAL AFRICAN PRAYER

Week 16

The Turtle Who Talked
—TRADITIONAL BUDDHIST STORY

Turtle was always talking. He talked so much the other animals in the pond became very annoyed with him and moved away when Turtle came near. They just didn't want to hear him talking anymore. So Turtle started talking to himself.

One day two geese came to visit the pond. Turtle started talking to them right away. He told the geese how beautiful their feathers were and went on and on about it. After a while, the geese were tired of Turtle's talking and they were about to fly away to another pond.

"Take me with you," Turtle pleaded. "It's so lonely here and you two have been so good to talk to."

"How can you possibly come with us?" the geese said to Turtle. "You cannot fly."

Turtle said, "Wait. I'll think of something." And then he said, "I know how. It's simple. We'll get a long, strong stick. Then you will each take one end in your beak and I'll bite hard in the middle. When you fly, all I'll have to do is hold on with my mouth."

The geese looked at the tall trees they would have to fly over to get to another pond. They said to Turtle, "What if you fall from such a height? Are you insane?"

"My mouth is so strong," Turtle said, "I won't fall."

The geese said, "Your mouth must be strong from so much talking, but you'll only be safe if you keep your mouth closed on the stick."

So the geese agreed to do their part and take Turtle up in the air. They got a long stick, Turtle bit down in the middle of it, and the geese flew up high over the tall trees.

Soon the children below saw an amazing sight in the sky—two geese carrying a turtle! "How smart those geese are!" they cried out. "They found a way to carry turtles! They're so smart!"

Turtle heard all of this and thought, "I'm the one who thought this up, not the geese. I'm the one who is so smart." He was so outraged with the children that he opened his mouth to shout at them. And Turtle fell straight down to the earth.

Bringing It Home

To Do This Week

❑ Is there someone in the family who annoys you by doing too much of something, like talking? Is there someone in the family that holds back because they're too quiet or shy?

❑ Pretend you're the geese. What would you do when Turtle talked on and on to you?

❑ Turtle talked too much and he did it at the wrong time. Think about something that you overdo. Spend the whole day doing less (or none if possible) of that one thing.

❑ Think about one thing you don't think you do often enough. Now do more of that one thing.

Blessing for Meals of the Week

The food is One
We who offer the food are One
The fire of hunger is also One
All action is One
We who understand this are One.

—TRADITIONAL HINDU BLESSING

Prayer for the Week

Most glorious of all who live forever, Zeus,
Nothing upon earth takes place without your will.
O, the unfortunate hungering to possess good things
Do not see God's laws and do not hear.
They could have a fine life and real riches;
Instead they rush without thinking after foolish things,
Like fame or gain, and get just the opposite.
But Zeus, giver of all gifts,
We pray you save your children from this endless misery.

—ADAPTED FROM PRAYER OF ANCIENT GREECE

Week 17

How Ijapa and Ojola Treated Each Other

—TRADITIONAL AFRICAN STORY

Ijapa the tortoise went on a long walk. He walked very far, Ijapa did, and got very tired. Ijapa was very hungry, too.

Ijapa came to the village where Ojola, the boa snake, lived. Ijapa thought, "I am so hungry, I will stop here. Ojola will surely give me food to eat."

Ijapa went to Ojola's house and Ojola welcomed him. They sat in the cool house and talked. Ijapa smelled food cooking in the other part of the house. Ojola said, "Come, let us get ready to eat together."

Ijapa went outside to prepare for the meal. When he came back, the food was placed in the center of the house and Ijapa smelled the aroma. But Ijapa could not reach the food. Ojola, the snake, was coiled all around it. Ojola's body was so long and his coils were piled so high that there was just no way Ijapa could get to the food. Ijapa got more and more hungry.

Ojola said, "Come sit with me and eat."

Ijapa said, "I would be very happy to sit and eat. But Ojola, why are you surrounding the meal?"

Ojola replied, "This is the way of the snakes. When we eat, we sit around the food like this." Ojola ate and ate of the food, but Ijapa could not get to it at all. Ojola finished eating at last. He said to Ijapa, "How good it is to eat with a friend."

Ijapa was even hungrier after the meal than when he came to Ojola's house. He felt much in his heart about what happened.

Ijapa decided to invite Ojola to his house for a meal on a feast day. Ijapa's wife prepared all the foods and Ijapa went out to weave a long tail for himself out of grass. He stuck it on with tree gum.

Ojola arrived to share the feast. Ijapa welcomed him and said, "You have come a long way and you are hungry." Ojola went to wash at a spring and when he returned to Ijapa's house, he saw Ijapa was already eating. Ijapa had coiled his long grass tail all around the food. Ojola could not get near enough to eat. Ijapa heartily ate the food.

Around and around Ojola went. He could not get to the food. "Ijapa," the snake said, "How is it that you used to be so short and now you are so very long?"

"One person learns from another," Ijapa said. Then Ojola remembered how it was when Ijapa had come to eat at his house.

Bringing It Home

To Do This Week

❏ Tell a story about when someone did not share with you. How did you feel? Tell a story about when you didn't share with someone else. How did you feel then?

❏ Pretend you are the characters in this story. How would you respond to the other not sharing food?

❏ Imagine you are Ijapa. How do you feel at the end of the story? Imagine you are Ojola. How do you feel at the end of the story?

❏ Imagine you are a friend of both Ijapa and Ojola. What would you say to them?

Blessing for Meals of the Week

O Great Spirit of our Ancestors, I raise my pipe to you,
To your messengers the four winds, and
To Mother Earth who provides for your children.
Let us learn to share all the good things that
You provide for us on this Earth.

—TRADITIONAL NATIVE AMERICAN PRAYER

Prayer for the Week

Your Lord knows well
What is in your souls
And whether you be of whole-heartedness.
Give to the poor and the traveler
But if you must turn away because of lack,
Expecting that the Lord will provide goods
For you later to give,
Then at least speak with kindness.

—ADAPTED FROM THE QUR'AN, HOLY BOOK OF ISLAM

Real Love

—TRADITIONAL STORY FROM HEBREW SCRIPTURES

When Solomon became king, he said to God, "I am like a little child; I do not know how to be a servant to all the people."

God appeared in a dream and asked Solomon, "What shall I give you?"

Solomon answered, "Give me a wise heart so I may tell who is good and who is bad among my people." And God was pleased to do this for Solomon.

Solomon was known as the wisest of the wise. He knew all about plants and flowers and how animals behaved. Some people believed he could even talk to the animals, and when they had a problem they came to the king for judgment.

One day, two women came to see King Solomon. There was a baby with them and they were fighting over it. Each one tried to take it away from the other! Finally one of the king's assistants held the baby while the two women told their story.

The first woman said to Solomon, "We live together in the same house and just a little while ago we both gave birth to babies. Mine was born first and then hers three days after. She accidentally rolled over on her baby in the night and the baby smothered to death. Then, while I was asleep, she got up at midnight. She took my baby and put her dead baby in place of mine. When I woke up I found the baby in my bed was dead. When I looked at the baby in the light I saw it was not mine."

The other woman said, "No, your baby is the one that died. Mine is the one that lives!"

Then Solomon said to the two mothers, "Both of you claim the living baby to be yours. I know a way to see which of you is true to the child."

The king called out, "Bring me a sword!" and a sword was brought to him. "Now," Solomon proclaimed, "cut the baby in two pieces and give half to each of the mothers."

Then the real mother cried out, "No! Do not kill the child. Give the baby to her." But the other woman said, "Go ahead. Let it be neither mine nor hers, but cut it in two."

Solomon ordered the swordsman to put down the sword. "The one who wants the child to live is the mother who loves him. Give the baby to her."

And everyone in all the land heard how Solomon had come to make this judgment. Surely the wisdom of God was in the heart of the king.

Bringing It Home

To Do This Week

❏ Write down one thing each person in your family has done to show that they love you. Write down one thing you've done for each person in your family that shows your love. Discuss what you have written.

❏ Imagine you are King Solomon. What would you do when you saw the two women fighting over the baby? Discuss your feelings about this story.

❏ Draw or paint a picture of someone in the family you love. Give something you hold dear to the person in your picture.

Blessing for Meals of the Week

O give thanks to the Lord
for his love is forever
for his wonderful works to the children of men!
For he fills the hungry soul with good things.

—FROM HEBREW SCRIPTURES

Prayer for the Week

May the wisdom of the snake be yours.
May the wisdom of the raven and the eagle be yours.
May your voice be as sweet as honey,
Like the voice of a child of the stars.

—ADAPTED FROM A TRADITIONAL CELTIC CHRISTIAN BLESSING

Week 19

A Cup of Water in the Desert

—TRADITIONAL SUFI STORY

A holy man named Aman made a journey to see the powerful Haroun Al-Rashid, the Caliph who governed a great empire. When Aman at last was allowed to see the Caliph, the simple man asked him a simple question. "If you were dying of thirst and alone in the desert, what would you give for a single cup of water?"

The Caliph did not even pause for a moment. "I'd give half my kingdom!" he shouted.

Aman nodded. Then quietly he asked, "And, what if the water you drank somehow filled you up so much you were about to burst? With your life in danger, O great Caliph, what would you give for a few pills that would cure your condition and keep your soul alive?"

"Surely I would give up the other half of my kingdom," Haroun Al-Rashid declared.

"Why then, O great Caliph," the saintly Aman inquired, "do you talk about what fantastic worth your kingdom has when you yourself are willing to give up the whole kingdom for a mere cup of water and a handful of pills?"

Bringing It Home

To Do This Week

❑ Imagine you are the holy Aman. Draw or paint a picture of what it's like living in the desert. Draw or paint a picture of what it's like being Caliph Haroun Al-Rashid, living in a magnificent palace. Show these to your family.

❑ Pretend you are Haroun. Do you have what is really important to you or are you missing something?

❑ What would you give to save yourself or a family member from a serious illness? Discuss what is of the greatest value to you.

❑ Once more, imagine you are Haroun and you are alone in the desert. What would you do then? Each family member take a turn.

Blessing for Meals of the Week

Bless, O Lord, the plants of the field,
That they may grow to fullness
And give much fruit.
And may the fruit of the earth
Help us to remember the fruit of the spirit
We should bring forth.

—TRADITIONAL COPTIC CHRISTIAN PRAYER OF EGYPT

Prayer for the Week

That which is holy,
may it be my offering.
That which is good,
may it be my offering.
The beautiful sparkling stone,
may it become my offering.
The beautiful grain of yellow corn,
may it be my offering.
The beautiful white shell,
may it be my offering.

—TRADITIONAL NATIVE AMERICAN PRAYER

Week 20

Warnings

— TRADITIONAL STORY FROM HEBREW SCRIPTURES

Moses had seen the burning flame of God high on the holy mountain. "Return to Egypt," God said to Moses, "and free my people from slavery."

Moses had grown up with Pharaoh, the ruler of Egypt, and he knew how stubborn and hard-hearted he could be. Moses was afraid that Pharaoh would not listen to God's command and let the people go.

God said, "Go. Your brother Aaron will join you and together you will show Pharaoh that God means to have his people, the Hebrews, be free." So Moses and Aaron went to Pharaoh.

Moses and Aaron had a special rod that God had given them. Aaron threw the stick down at Pharaoh's feet and it turned into a snake. But Pharaoh only laughed at them. "My magicians can do the same thing," he said. Even when the snake from Aaron's rod swallowed up the ones the Egyptians made, Pharaoh would not let the people go.

Nine more times Moses went to see Pharaoh just as God had told him to do. Moses gave Pharaoh God's message, "Let my people go," and told him that terrible things would happen if Pharaoh refused. But Pharaoh did not listen to these warnings.

So plagues came to Egypt. The great River Nile was turned to a bloody red and many fish died. Frogs swarmed in the land, hopping into people's houses and even into their beds. Stinging flies were everywhere.

Then the cows all got sick and died and nearly all the grain was eaten up by flying grasshoppers. There was very little food left in Egypt.

The Hebrews were not harmed in any way. God wanted Pharaoh and the Egyptians to know that the plagues were only happening to them and that when the people of God were freed, the plagues would stop. But still Pharaoh would not change his mind.

Then a great darkness came to Egypt. Even though it was daytime, there was no sunlight at all. This terribly frightened the Egyptians, but Pharaoh would not let the people of God go free.

Finally God gave a last warning. He told Moses, "Tonight Pharaoh's heart will no longer be hard against you. Tonight an angel will come to visit, and only in the houses marked with the sign of blood will the first-born children live." The Hebrews marked their houses but the Egyptians did not. The first-born children of Egypt died in the night and all of Egypt cried with grief.

Then Pharaoh let the people go.

Bringing It Home

To Do This Week

❏ Pretend you are Moses. What would you do when Pharaoh wouldn't listen to you the first time?

❏ Draw or paint a picture of one or more of the signs God used through Moses to warn Pharaoh.

❏ Tell a story about when you received a warning and didn't listen. Tell a story about when you received a warning and you did listen.

❏ Imagine God's angel is coming to your house. Draw or paint a picture to show the angel that you are one of God's children and that the angel must pass over your house.

Blessing for Meals of the Week

As plentiful as the grass that grows,
Or the sand on the shore,
So the blessings of the King of Grace
On every soul that was, that is, or will be.

—TRADITIONAL IRISH BLESSING

Prayer for the Week

In the name of God, most compassionate, most merciful
Praise be to God,
Lord of all, most merciful one
Ruler of the Day of Judgment
You are the One we worship
And we plead to you for help.
Guide us in the straight way
The way of those graced by you
Not of those with whom you are angry
Not of those who wander off.

— TRADITIONAL PRAYER FROM THE QUR'AN, HOLY BOOK OF ISLAM

Week 21

What Does Everybody Have?
—TRADITIONAL AFRICAN STORY

Morning and Evening were brothers, sons of Mahu. Mahu was God of all the people, but he did not treat Morning and Evening with equal generosity. Morning was the one born first, so Mahu gave him many people to rule over and a great number of precious things also. Evening, the younger one, got a calabash with two kinds of beads—nana and azumun—contained inside it. These two kinds of beads were the only things that Mahu had not given to his older son, Morning. Morning had riches of all sorts, but of nana and azumun he had none.

One day Morning fell sick and the doctor was called to cure him. The doctor said there was only one treatment for Morning's illness; he needed a nana bead and an azumun bead. Then Morning would be well again.

Since Morning had none of these beads, his people went out to get them. But nobody in all the land had any. Evening was the only one who had nana and azumun beads.

"How much will you give me for these beads?" Evening asked the people his brother Morning sent.

"We will pay one hundred precious cowrie shells for each one," they answered.

So Evening sold them the beads and they left. When Morning was cured, Evening began to think. "If Morning were to get sick over and over again," Evening thought, "I could get a great many precious cowrie shells."

Evening remembered that when Morning passed a calabash plant, the leaves curled up. So Evening placed wholly open calabash leaves in Morning's path. When Morning's feet touched them, he became ill right away.

In this way, Evening made Morning sick as often as he wished. Morning had to keep giving his brother cowrie shells and after a while Evening had all of them. He became the richest one in the land and the people looked at Evening as their king.

Bringing It Home

To Do This Week

❑ Pretend you are Morning. What does it feel like to have all your riches but you and your brother don't see each other?

❑ Imagine you are one of Evening's friends. What would you say to him if you found out he was making his brother sick?

❑ At the beginning of the story do you think Morning thought there was anything wrong in his life? What about at the end? At the beginning of the story, do you think Evening thought he had problems? What about at the end?

Blessing for Meals of the Week

O God, you have made heaven and earth.
You have given me all the good things of the earth.
Here is your share, God.
Take it from me!

—TRADITIONAL AFRICAN BLESSING

Prayer for the Week

O God, Agni, keep us from grief and swallow up
Our enemies with your hottest fire.
Be you a mighty fort with a hundred walls for us.
Keep us, morning and evening,
From sorrow and from the wicked.

—TRADITIONAL HINDU PRAYER

Week 22

The Fish and the Snake

—TRADITIONAL BUDDHIST STORY

Once there lived in the sacred River Ganges a big water snake. He used to hide underneath a rock and look for a fish swimming by. Then the snake would dart out from under the rock, grab the fish in its mouth, and eat it. The snake always took the fish by surprise and always got to eat it.

One day when the snake was swimming in the river, he saw a whole school of very small fish eating their meal together. "How fortunate I am today!" the snake said to himself. "I have a whole lot of fish right here for me to eat."

And the snake opened his mouth very wide and swam into the middle of all the fish. He was expecting to catch the fish as easily as he usually did. "I'm going to eat them all up," the snake said.

But before he could eat even one of them, the whole school of fish surrounded the snake and started biting him. They bit the snake from head to tail and made him bleed all over.

The snake was afraid that the tiny fish would end up killing him, so he swam away as quickly as he could to the riverbank.

The snake was in great pain and lay down to rest. Near him, he saw a big green frog who was lying on a rock and getting warm in the afternoon sun. The snake called out, "My dear sir, just look at what those fish did to me. Does it seem right to you that they should attack me in such a way?"

The big green frog looked at the bloody snake and croaked out in reply, "You are used to sneaking up on the fish one at a time and eating them up. Now you thought you could gobble them up all at once by swimming among them. You are just a bully, but you found out that together the fish are stronger than you. Now they have gotten the better of you!"

Bringing It Home

To Do This Week

❏ Draw or paint a picture of the snake. If you were a fish swimming alone, would the snake scare you? Tell a story about how someone tried to bully you.

❏ Pretend you are a fish that somehow got away from the snake. What would you do? Imagine you were a friend of the fish that got away. What would you do when you heard about what the snake was doing?

❏ Think about what the frog said. Do you think the snake agreed with him? Do you think the fish agreed with him?

❏ Do something today—moving something big and heavy, for example—that only the whole family together can do.

Blessing for Meals of the Week

Greetings to you, O God
Who provides food for the body and soul.
You have been kind and given what is before us.
We thank you.
Please bless the loving hands that prepared this meal and
We who are to enjoy it.

—TRADITIONAL HINDU BLESSING

Prayer for the Week

The Lord make his face to shine upon you,
and be gracious unto you:
The Lord lift up his countenance upon you,
and give you peace.

—TRADITIONAL PRAYER FROM HEBREW SCRIPTURES

Week 23

How Does It Look to You?

One day a farmer went out from his farm. He closed the gate to the yard where all the animals stayed, meaning to return in a short while.

But days and days went by and the farmer did not come back. All the animals became very hungry and thirsty. Even the rooster lost the energy to crow.

The animals sat motionless in the shade of a big tree. They were trying to stay alive until the farmer gave them food and water again.

But the peacock gathered all his remaining strength together. He rose up, opened his multi-colored tail, and strutted before all the other animals.

"Mama," asked a little chicken, "why is the peacock showing off his tail like that?"

"Because the peacock is so proud of the way he looks," she answered. "My child, this is a fault that will only disappear with death."

—FABLE OF LEONARDO DA VINCI

* * *

A deer came to a pool to drink, and stopped to look at his image in the water. When he saw his mighty antlers, the deer swelled with pride. When he saw his legs reflected in the water, the deer was sorry that they appeared to be so skinny and weak.

While he was thinking these thoughts, a lion suddenly ran right at him. The deer took off and quickly outran the lion chasing him, for a deer's strength is in his legs and a lion's strength is in the heart; so as long as the deer kept running on the plain, he kept ahead of the lion.

But when the deer ran into the forest, his antlers got stuck on some tree branches and the lion caught up to him. Just as the lion was about to kill him, the deer sadly said to himself, "How strange things are! My scrawny legs almost got me away to safety, and my magnificent antlers cost me my life!"

— GREEK FABLE OF AESOP

Bringing It Home

To Do This Week

❏ The peacock was proud of his tail and the deer of his antlers. Draw or paint a picture of something about yourself that makes you very proud. Show everyone your picture. Then talk both about what you are proud of and ashamed of.

❏ Pretend you are the peacock. How do you think the other animals feel about you and your tail? Pretend you're the deer. What do you think the lion felt about your legs?

❏ Share a story about someone you know who has a disability. What is special about her or him?

❏ Using the things you talked about this week, make up a short fable about yourself. Share it with your family.

Blessing for Meals of the Week

Go your way and
Eat your bread with joy and
Drink with a joyful heart
For God accepts what you do.

—BLESSING FROM HEBREW SCRIPTURES

Prayer for the Week

May the Great Spirit send his best gifts to you.
May the Sun father and Moon mother
Shine their softest light on you.
May the four winds of heaven blow gently upon you and
Upon all who share your heart and home.

—TRADITIONAL NATIVE AMERICAN PRAYER

When the Cat Came to Muhammad

— TRADITIONAL MUSLIM STORY

The prophet Muhammad (peace be upon him) was reading from the Qur'an, the holy book, to a large group of eager listeners in the desert. A sickly cat walked up to Muhammad (peace be upon him), sat down on the hem of his very precious robe, and went to sleep.

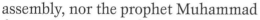

All day the prophet Muhammad (peace be upon him) shared talk with the believers, the sun rising to its greatest strength and falling again, and none of the assembly, nor the prophet Muhammad (peace be upon him) moved from this place. The cat as well remained asleep and still, healing in the way cats do, in the protection of the prophet Muhammad (peace be upon him) and the softness of his robe.

At last, the day was coming to its end and all, along with the prophet Muhammad (peace be upon him), were now to return to their dwelling places for the night.

Without a word, the prophet Muhammad (peace be upon him) took a knife, cut off the hem of his robe on which the sick cat still lay sleeping, destroying the finest of robes, and left the cat undisturbed.

Bringing It Home

To Do This Week

❑ Draw or paint a picture of Mohammed's wonderful robe, then draw or paint a picture of the cat at the end of the day.

❑ Pretend you are Muhammad and you are giving an important speech. What would you do when the sick cat walked up to you? Pretend you are one of the people listening to the holy prophet. What would you do when the cat sat on his robe?

❑ Share a story about when you asked somebody to help you. Share a story about when a person or an animal needed your help.

❑ Think and talk about a way to help someone in your neighborhood, school, or workplace.

Blessing for Meals of the Week

This food we eat is for the Three Treasures,
For our teachers, family and all beings.
The first portion is to avoid all evil.
The second is to do all good.
The third is to save all beings.
We eat this food and awaken with everyone.

—ADAPTED FROM A BUDDHIST CHANT

Prayer for the Week

O God, O Sun, the cattle rest in the fields,
The plants and the trees are growing,
The birds fly above the wetlands.
All creatures find life when you shine upon them.

—ANCIENT EGYPTIAN HYMN

Week 25

What the Twins Wanted

—TRADITIONAL STORY FROM HEBREW SCRIPTURES

Isaac was the son of Abraham, the first of the Hebrew fathers to be blessed by God. When Abraham died, the blessing had passed to Isaac and Isaac in turn was to bestow it on his oldest son.

But Isaac's wife Rebekah gave birth to not one, but two sons. These twins, Esau and Jacob, were as different as they could be.

The older one, Esau, was born covered with fiery red hair. He grew up to be a wild and adventurous young man who wanted only to hunt. Jacob was born holding onto his brother's heel, and he liked staying home and learning.

Esau was the father's favorite. He brought the old man the good hearty meat he had hunted and killed. Jacob was the mother's favorite and she taught him many things.

One day Esau was out hunting and Jacob was home, cooking a pot of lentil stew. Esau had been gone the whole day and was hungry as a bear. When he came in, Esau shouted at Jacob, "Give me some of that stew right now before I faint!"

And Jacob said, "I will if you trade it for the blessing from our father."

Esau grunted. "I'll give it to you. I'm dying from hunger anyway. Just get me some food!"

Isaac grew to be very old. He had become blind and was soon to die. He asked Esau to hunt a deer and cook the delicious meal Isaac so loved. "Bring it to me one last time," Isaac said to Esau. "I want to eat of it so that my soul may bless you before I die."

Rebekah heard Isaac's request of Esau and she wanted her son Jacob, not Esau, to get the blessing, so she told Jacob her plan. "While Esau is out hunting," Rebekah said, "I'll cook the special meal he wants and you'll go in disguised as Esau and bring it to him. Then he will give you the blessing!"

"But Esau is all hairy, and I am not," Jacob said. "Our father will know."

Rebekah calmed Jacob. "We'll dress you in Esau's clothes and put goat skins on your hands and arms."

It worked. Old, blind Isaac was fooled into believing it was his son Esau he touched. He gave Jacob the blessing.

When Esau came in later, he realized what had happened. Esau was angry and afraid that there was nothing left for him. "Have you not a blessing for me, too, Father?" Esau asked.

And Isaac blessed Esau too. He said, "The fortress of the earth and the waters of heaven will be for you. Someday," he told Esau, "you will have as good a life as your brother."

Bringing It Home

To Do This Week

❏ The blessing was deeply important to both Jacob and Esau. Draw or paint a picture of something important to you, something you really want to have. Think about what you are willing to do to get what you want.

❏ Tell a story about something you really wanted that you ended up getting. How did it turn out? Was there ever something you really wanted that you didn't get? How did it turn out?

❏ Talk about each character in this story and what happened to that person. Which person in the story do you think was the most blessed and the happiest?

Blessing for Meals of the Week

May the abundance of this table
Never fail and never be less.
Thanks to the blessings of God,
Who has fed us and satisfied our needs.
To him be glory forever. Amen.

—TRADITIONAL ARMENIAN CHRISTIAN BLESSING

Prayer for the Week

The one whose mind is like a rock
Stands unmoved and never shakes.
Delightful things do not make this one hotter,
Nor does provocation make this one angry.
How can trouble come
To one who has trained his mind in such a noble way?

—TRADITIONAL BUDDHIST TEACHING

The Lotus Tree

—MYTH OF ANCIENT GREECE

One day Dryope and her sister Iole went to the pool. They wished to gather flowers in honor of the nymphs; divine spirits who dwelled on the earth.

Dryope was carrying her little son in her arms. When she saw a lotus tree blooming with bright flowers, she stopped to pick some for her little boy because she knew he liked these pretty flowers so much.

But as soon as she picked the blossoms, Dryope saw a horrible sight. Drops of blood were running down the flower stems! The tree was not what it seemed to be. It was really the nymph Lotis who was hiding from an attacker and had become the tree herself. Dryope was terribly frightened to see Lotis bleeding and she tried to run away. But her feet stuck like roots in the ground.

As her sister Iole watched, Dryope's body began turning to tree bark. Iole could do nothing but go and get Dryope's husband and father.

By the time they returned, only Dryope's face was not yet fully covered. The two men ran and hugged the tree trunk, still warm with their beloved Dryope's blood. They cried so much, their tears ran down to water the tree.

Dryope had only a few moments to talk before her mouth became part of the lotus tree. She told them that she had meant no harm and begged them to bring her child to the tree often. "Let him come and play in the shade," Dryope said. "Some day you will tell him the story and he will know his mother is here in this tree."

Dryope had one last important thing to say. "Tell the child never to pick flowers, for any bush or tree may really be a divine spirit."

These were Dryope's final words. The bark covered her face and she became a tree forever.

Bringing It Home

To Do This Week

❏ Draw or paint a picture of the lotus tree and its bright flowers.

❏ Imagine you are Dryope. How do you feel when the tree starts bleeding? Tell a story about when you found out you had hurt someone. What did you do?

❏ Tell someone in your family about something they did without knowing it that hurt you. As each of you takes a turn, the others just listen.

❏ Imagine again you are Dryope and you have been the tree for a long time. If you could tell your son anything more, what would it be?

❏ Go and touch a tree. Tell the tree you are sorry that so many trees all over the earth are being hurt and destroyed.

Blessing for Meals of the Week

I am like a green olive tree
Growing in the house of God.
I trust in the loving-kindness of God
Forever.

—FROM HEBREW SCRIPTURES

Prayer for the Week

May the ax be far away from you.
May the fire be far away from you.
May there be rain and not great storms.
Lord of Trees, may you be blessed.
Lord of Trees, may I be blessed.

—TRADITIONAL HINDU PRAYER

Everyone Is Beautiful

—TRADITIONAL NATIVE AMERICAN STORY

One day the Creator said, "I'm going to watch the children playing in the village." The children were laughing and singing, but the Creator was sad in his heart for he thought, "Someday they will grow old. Their skin will become wrinkled like their grandmothers' and grandfathers', and they will lose their teeth. The young hunters will get weak and the beautiful girls will become ugly. And all the bright, colorful, wonderful flowers they are playing with will lose their colors. The leaves will fall to the ground, too," the Creator said to himself. And his heart was even sadder.

The sun was still shining and it was bright. The Creator saw the sunlight all golden, the sky so blue, the white corn, the yellow leaves, and all the colors of the flowers. He smiled and said, "I'll take these colors and I'll make something with them, something for the children to see and make them happy, and this will bring joy to my heart."

The Creator took a bit of sunlight, some sky blue, the white color of corn, the dark gray shadows the running children made, yellow from the falling leaves, pine needle green, black from a beautiful girl's long hair, and purple, orange, and red from growing flowers. He put all this in a special bag. After doing all that, he put in the songs of the birds, too.

The children were playing in a field and the Creator said to them, "Children, I have a gift for you. Look in this bag and you'll see."

Many, many colored butterflies flew out of the bag when the children opened it; so many they filled the sky. They fluttered from flower to flower and danced on top of the children's heads. The children had never seen such beautiful creatures. There was joy in their hearts.

The beautiful butterflies began to sing. This too made the children happy. A songbird heard the butterflies singing their songs and flew to the Creator. The bird sat on the Creator's shoulder and spoke harshly in his ear. "You promised the birds, every one of us, would have a song of our own. Now you have given them away to these new creatures. It is not a good way. These new creatures are full of beautiful colors. Haven't you given them enough?"

"You speak the truth," the Creator told the bird. "The songs belong to you, one song for each of you just as I said it would be."

Bringing It Home

To Do This Week

❑ The butterflies have beautiful colors; what is beautiful about you? Draw a picture showing how beautiful you are. The birds have the gift of song; what special gifts or talents do you have? Show one of your talents or gifts; either draw it on the same paper, or demonstrate your talent to your family.

❑ Tell each other (parents and children) three things that are beautiful about each one, and name three gifts or talents you see that each family member has.

❑ Pretend you're the butterfly. How do you feel at the end of the story? How does the songbird feel at the end of the story? How does the Creator feel at the end of the story?

Blessing for Meals of the Week

We thank the sun,
We thank the earth,
We thank the rain,
We thank the farmers,
We thank the people at the store,
And we thank the One
Who made the food
That gives us life today.

—INSPIRED BY A TRADITIONAL BUDDHIST BLESSING

Prayer for the Week

I am the wind that blows upon the sea.
I am the wave on the ocean.
I am the rays of the sun.
I am the light of the moon and stars.
I am the strength of trees growing.
I am fish swimming.
I am the courage of the wild pigs fighting.
I am the speed of the deer running.
I am the big and mighty oak tree.
And I am the thoughts of all people
Who praise my beauty and grace.

—ADAPTED FROM A CELTIC CHRISTIAN PRAYER CHANT

Week 28

Why Fight?

—TRADITIONAL BUDDHIST STORY

The Buddha's people, the Shakyas, and their neighbors, the Kolis, were just about to fight.

A river ran between their two cities and both peoples needed the water from the river to raise crops in their fields. A dam had been built so that everyone got enough. But then, a great drought came and the water almost all dried up. There was very little left and both sides claimed the water was theirs.

The Shakyas and the Kolis in the area started calling each other very bad names and cursing one another as well. Soon the princes of both countries heard of the dispute and of course the stories told made things look much worse than they really were. But the princes were outraged. They both called their armies to battle.

The Shakya and Koli soldiers marched to the river and faced off. Though he was far away, Buddha saw in his mind that the war was just about to begin. He sent himself through the sky and came to the battle-ground. When they saw him, the Shakyas cast down their swords for they honored Buddha as the jewel of their people. The Kolis did as well.

In a light manner, Buddha asked them, since they were gathered at the river, "Have you come to celebrate a water festival?"

"No," they told him. "We came to fight."

Buddha asked what caused them to fight. The princes were not really sure, so they asked the generals, who were not sure themselves. The generals in turn asked the other officers and no one really knew until the farmers of the land told Buddha, "We're fighting about this water."

Buddha asked them then about the water and about men—what was the value of each? They said that the value of water was very little, but the value of men was very great indeed. "Why, then, do you prepare to fight and waste the greater for the lesser?" Buddha simply put forth.

The Shakyas and the Kolis called off the war.

Bringing It Home

To Do This Week

❑ Draw or paint a picture of the river running between the two cities.

❑ Share a story about when someone started calling you names. What did you do? Have you called someone names? Tell the story. What happened afterwards?

❑ Share a story about a fight you saw starting. What did you do?

❑ Talk about the last argument you had with someone in your family. As each person shares, everyone else listens.

❑ Go somewhere where you'll be alone and scream as loud as you want.

Blessing for Meals of the Week

O Lord, to our prayers we add
Our sincere thanks for all your mercies,
For our very being and for our ability to reason,
For our health and for our friends,
For our clothing and for our food,
And all the other pleasant and good things of life.

—ADAPTED FROM A TRADITIONAL CHRISTIAN ENGLISH PRAYER

Prayer for the Week

How good and how pleasant it is
When brothers live as one!
Like the dew on the mountain of Hermon,
Like the dew that falls on the holy mountains of Zion,
For the Lord gave the blessing of life evermore.

— TRADITIONAL PRAYER FROM HEBREW SCRIPTURES

Week 29

Let's Wait and See

—TRADITIONAL CHINESE TAOIST STORY

A poor farmer's prize horse disappeared one day, and was seen heading for the country of the barbarians. The other farmers, poor like him, knew how much the horse meant to the family and expressed their sympathy. The farmer said only, "Let's wait and see. How do you know this isn't good fortune?"

A few months passed. Lo and behold, the farmer's horse came back, bringing with it another horse. The new horse was very strong. The neighbors congratulated the farmer for his good luck. The old farmer said, "Let's wait and see. How do you know this doesn't mean a disaster is coming?" The peasants merely shook their heads and went back to their work.

After a while, the two horses became father and mother to many fine horses and the family became very rich. The farmer's son, with leisure time now on his hands, took a fancy to riding his magnificent horse, and one day he fell off and broke his hip. Once again came the other farmers to offer condolences and to wish him a quick recovery for his son. The farmer told them, "Let's wait and see. How do you know this is not a good thing?"

Well, the hip did not heal well, and the son became lame as a result. Some time went by, and the barbarians crossed the border into the farmer's land and attacked. All able-bodied young men were required to fight in the war. Nine out of ten of them died. The farmer's son, lame as he was, stayed home and alive.

Bringing It Home

To Do This Week

❏ Is there anything that you worry about happening in the future? Share just one thing with your family.

❏ Share a story about something happening to you that you thought was bad. How did it turn out? Do the same with a story about something happening that you thought was good.

❏ What do you think will happen next in the story?

Blessing for Meals of the Week

My God, live forever.
My God, may you allow me to smell the sweet smell
of your life that has no end.
My God, we are never full of your life.

—TRADITIONAL AFRICAN PRAYER

Prayer for the Week

Let nothing upset you,
Let nothing frighten you.
Everything is changing;
God alone is changeless.
Patience achieves the aim.
Who has God lacks nothing;
God alone fills all needs.

—PRAYER OF SAINT TERESA OF AVILA

King David and the Spider
—TRADITIONAL JEWISH STORY

When King David was still a boy watching over his father's sheep, he often came upon spiders' webs strung across tree branches and shining in the sun. David thought the spiders were wonderful to weave such webs, but he could see no use for them.

David decided to ask God about it. "Why, O Creator of the world, did you make spiders? You can't even wear their webs as clothing!"

God answered David, "A day will come when you will need the work of this creature. Then you will thank me."

David grew up and became a courageous warrior. He defeated the giant Goliath and many enemies of the people of Israel. He married King Saul's daughter and the people adored him as the greatest man in the land.

King Saul was jealous and afraid of David and sent his soldiers to kill him. David ran away to the wilderness. He hoped King Saul's fit of anger would pass and David would be safe to return. But King Saul's men kept chasing him.

At last, the soldiers were very close. David ran into a cave to hide. He heard the footsteps of the men and knew that they would soon find him. David was so afraid his bones shook and hurt.

But then David saw a big spider at the front of the cave. Very quickly, it was spinning a web all the way across the opening. Just before the soldiers came up to the cave, the spider finished the web. As the men started to enter the cave, they ran into the web. "Look," they said, "This web is unbroken. If David were here, he'd have torn the web to pieces. He must be hiding somewhere else. Let's go!"

So because of the spider, David's life was saved. David understood that God was wise and thanked God for creating all the creatures, including the spiders.

Bringing It Home

To Do This Week

❏ Imagine you are a spider. Describe the webs you make and what good they are to you and others.

❏ Together, go look at a spider's web. Then draw or paint a picture of both a spider and a web.

❏ Tell a story about when you really needed help and someone you didn't expect—like the spider—ended up helping you.

❏ Name three different animals. Why do you think God created them?

❏ Pretend that David asked you, "Why has God created you?" What is your answer?

Blessing for Meals of the Week

The Lord is my shepherd,
I shall not want.
He brings my soul back to life and
He leads me on the right path for his name's sake.
You prepare a table before me.
Even when my enemies are all around me,
Surely goodness and loving kindness
Will follow me all the days of my life.

—ADAPTED FROM A PRAYER OF HEBREW SCRIPTURES

Prayer for the Week

I have been to the end of the earth.
I have been to the end of the waters.
I have been to the end of the sky.
I have been to the end of the mountains.
I have found none that were not my friends.

—TRADITIONAL NATIVE AMERICAN PRAYER SONG

Week 31

The Lion's Enemy

—TRADITIONAL HINDU STORY

In India long ago there lived a lion who ruled the jungle. Just to show all the other animals how powerful he was, the lion hunted and killed even when his belly was full. The animals were terribly afraid of him.

So the animals of the jungle got together to talk about how they could get the lion to stop killing so many of them and agreed to a plan. Each day one animal would go to the lion and offer to be the lion's meal. The animals hoped the lion would then be satisfied.

When they went to the lion, they said, "This will be so much easier for you. You won't have to hunt, but just eat the animal who comes to you." The surprised lion agreed, but he roared loudly and said, "The animal must come at my regular mealtime. I, the king of the jungle, will not wait for anyone."

The next day the old rabbit was the animal chosen to be the lion's meal. He walked slowly, stopping to chew on bits of grass and talk to friends along the way. The wise old rabbit had plenty of time to think. When he finally approached the lion's place, the sun was setting. It was very, very late, far past the lion's mealtime, and the lion was very, very hungry.

The lion roared in anger at the rabbit. "Why are you so late?"

The rabbit answered, "O great King, it is not my fault. A most terrible lion prevented me from getting here on time. I was very lucky to escape with my life!" The lion paused to listen. "Yes," the rabbit went on, "I see him before me still. That long thick mane just like you, that strong, powerful body, just like you, and those nasty sharp claws and teeth, just like you!"

The lion became very angry. "Another lion in my jungle!" he shouted. "Take me to see him."

The rabbit said, "Certainly, my king, follow me," and the rabbit led the lion to a well. The rabbit pointed and said, "Look, that terrible lion is right down there!"

The lion looked down and, seeing his reflection in the well, believed it was his enemy—the new lion that the rabbit had described to him. He let out a terrific roar. The roar echoed right back to him and the lion asked, "Who are you?" His own question echoed back and in answer the lion roared, "I am king of this jungle!" This too was the answer from the lion in the well. "How dare you come here!" the lion raged, but he heard the same threat, "How dare you come here!" from the well.

The lion was beside himself with anger. He jumped into the well to kill his enemy, and drowned.

The rabbit returned home and told all the animals how the lion had attacked his own reflection in the well. The lion was dead and would never attack any of them again.

Bringing It Home

To Do This Week

❑ Imagine you are the lion. What would you do when the rabbit told you about the other lion he had seen?

❑ Do you think it was hard for the lion to go off looking for a fight with the other lion?

❑ Imagine you are one of the animals in the jungle. Draw or paint a picture of the lion. Imagine you are the lion looking into the well. Draw or paint a picture of the reflection you see. Show these pictures to your family and discuss them.

Blessing for Meals of the Week

In peace let us eat this food
Which the Lord has provided for us.
Blessed be the Lord in
His gifts. Amen.

—traditional Armenian Christian blessing

Prayer for the Week

O Wakan-Tanka,
the Great Spirit that moves through the universe,
Help me understand the teachings in every leaf and every stone.
O Wakan-Tanka,
I ask for strength not to be greater than my relations
but to conquer the enemy in myself.
May I come to you with a true heart and clear eyes.
With honor may my spirit come to you.

—adapted from a traditional Native American prayer

Week 32

How Do You Learn Common Sense?

—TRADITIONAL BURMESE BUDDHIST STORY

He was a young man of sixteen and very tall, so the other boys nicknamed him Master Tall. Master Tall was seen as one lacking intelligence. Still, he was sent by his father to the monastery, as were other boys by their fathers. But although he was obedient to the monks and popular with the other boys of the monastery, he learned nothing.

It was now time for him to leave the monastery and earn a living, but his father could not get him any work outside, and he was practically useless on his father's farm. Finally he became a herdsman, caring for his father's three buffaloes. Poor Master Tall found it impossible to tell one buffalo from another. Once he had put his father's buffaloes to pasture, he could not find them among the buffaloes of other herdsmen. Discovering Master Tall's failing, the other herdsmen took advantage. They lay at ease on the grass, playing on their reed pipes or laughing and joking, and whenever they saw a buffalo going astray or wandering onto a piece of farmland, they shouted, "Master Tall, Master Tall, there goes your buffalo!" Master Tall, thinking every buffalo that strayed was his, spent the whole long day chasing and catching the buffaloes. When evening came, he had to wait until the other herdsmen had taken away all their buffaloes, leaving the three belonging to his father, so that when he arrived home, it was late. This happened for many days, until his anxious father made inquiries and discovered the trick played on his son.

99

So the next day the fond father placed wreaths made of palm leaves on the horns of his three buffaloes and said, "Now, my son, look at the buffaloes carefully and remember that only a buffalo which has a wreath of palm leaves around his horns is your responsibility. Do not tire yourself by herding all the buffaloes of the village."

That morning, whenever the other herdsmen shouted, "Hey, Master Tall, there goes your animal," Master Tall glanced at the straying buffalo's horns, and if he saw no wreath on its horns, he just sat down and took no further notice. However, by midday Master Tall's secret had been discovered by the other boys, who then put wreaths of palm leaves on the horns of their buffaloes too, with the result that poor Master Tall spent the entire afternoon chasing all the stray buffaloes.

He was late again in reaching home, and to his anxious father, who had been waiting for him at the gate of his house, Master Tall complained, "Father, all was well in the morning, but at midday wreaths of palm leaves sprouted on the horns of the other buffaloes also."

Bringing It Home

To Do This Week

❏ Take a piece of fruit—one that will last the whole week—and place it on a table. Each day, each member of the family should touch, hold, and smell the fruit for five minutes. Listen to the silence or the sound of the fruit.

❏ Imagine you are Master Tall. What would you do when the other boys told him every one of the wandering buffaloes was his?

❏ Imagine you are Master Tall's father. What would you do when Master Tall came home after chasing all the buffaloes again?

❏ At the end of the week, each person tastes the fruit. Share your understanding of what the fruit is.

Blessing for Meals of the Week

*O God, who has blessed the earth and made it
to be fruitful and bring forth what we need for life,
and has commanded us to work in quietness,
Bless the labors of those who work the fields that we may harvest the
fruits of the earth.*

—ADAPTED FROM A TRADITIONAL CHRISTIAN ENGLISH PRAYER

Prayer for the Week

*I bow to the One who has no color,
I bow to the One who has no beginning.
I bow to the One who is without fault,
I bow to the One who is beyond our understanding.*

—ADAPTED FROM A SIKH PRAYER

Just the Way You Like It

—TRADITIONAL JEWISH STORY

A poor man lived with his wife and six children in a very small one-room house. They were always getting in each other's way and there was so little space they could hardly breathe!

Finally the man could stand it no more. He talked to his wife and asked her what to do. "Go see the rabbi," she told him, and after arguing a while, he went.

The rabbi greeted him and asked, "I see something is troubling you. Whatever it is, you can tell me."

And so the poor man told the rabbi how miserable things were at home with him, his wife, and the six children all eating and living and sleeping in one room. The poor man told the rabbi, "We're even starting to yell and fight with each other. Life couldn't be worse."

The rabbi thought very deeply about the poor man's problem. Then he said, "Do exactly as I tell you and things will get better. Do you promise?"

"I promise," the poor man said.

The rabbi then asked the poor man a strange question. "Do you own any animals?"

"Yes," he said. "I have one cow, one goat, and some chickens."

"Good," the rabbi said. "When you get home, take all the animals into your house to live with you."

The poor man was astonished to hear this advice from the rabbi, but he had promised to do exactly what the rabbi said. So he went home and took all the farm animals into the tiny one-room house.

The next day the poor man ran back to see the rabbi. "What have you done to me, Rabbi?" he cried. "It's awful. I did what you told me and the animals are all over the house! Rabbi, help me!"

The rabbi listened and said calmly, "Now go home and take the chickens back outside."

The poor man did as the rabbi said, but hurried back again the next day. "The chickens are gone, but Rabbi, the goat!" he moaned. "The goat is smashing up all the furniture and eating everything in sight!"

The good rabbi said, "Go home and remove the goat and may God bless you."

So the poor man went home and took the goat outside. But he ran back again to see the rabbi, crying and wailing. "What a nightmare you have brought to my house, Rabbi! With the cow it's like living in a stable! Can human beings live with an animal like this?"

The rabbi said sweetly, "My friend, you are right. May God bless you. Go home now and take the cow out of your house." And the poor man went quickly home and took the cow out of the house.

The next day he came running back to the rabbi again. "O Rabbi," he said with a big smile on his face, "we have such a good life now. The animals are all out of the house. The house is so quiet and we've got room to spare! What a joy!"

Bringing It Home

To Do This Week

❑ Draw or paint a picture of the poor man's tiny house with everyone in his family living there. Draw or paint a picture of your house with everyone in your family in it.

❑ Think about your biggest complaint and what the rabbi would tell you if he heard it. Today, follow the rabbi's advice and share with the whole family what happened.

❑ Imagine you are the man in the story. At the end, what would you say to a friend who complained about how bad life was?

Blessing for Meals of the Week

Look! Our Mother Earth is here.
Look! We see in Mother Earth the growing fields.
Look! We see in Mother Earth the growing trees.
Look! She gives us of her fruit.
Her power truly she gives to us.
Give thanks to Mother Earth.

—ADAPTED FROM A TRADITIONAL NATIVE AMERICAN SONG

Prayer for the Week

O Give thanks unto the Lord
For the Lord is good and his mercy is forever.
Let the ones the Lord has rescued and
Gathered from all lands,
Who wandered in the wilderness
With no place to live,
Who cried unto the Lord in their trouble
Praise the Lord for his goodness and
Wonderful works to the children of humankind.

—ADAPTED FROM HEBREW SCRIPTURES

Week 34

The First to Get the Bow

—TRADITIONAL NATIVE AMERICAN STORY

In the very beginning, the Creator Kareya made the world. He made the fishes of the ocean first, then he made all the animals that live on the earth, and after the fishes and the animals at last Kareya made a man. Kareya made all the creatures so that no one was more powerful than another and no one was seen as better or worse than any other. This is how Kareya made all the creatures.

One day Kareya spoke to the man and told him, "I am going to call together all the animals. You go make as many bows and arrows as there are animals in the world. You will give the animal that should have the most power the longest bow and arrow and the one that should have the least power the shortest bow and arrow."

In nine days, the man made a bow and arrow for every animal Kareya had created, and Kareya called all the animals together to listen to him. "Tomorrow," Kareya said, "the man will come and give you a bow. The animal who gets the longest bow will have the greatest power of all."

105

They all wanted the longest bow, but Coyote was the only one who believed he knew how to get it. He thought if he were the first animal the man saw in the morning that he, Coyote, would get the longest bow.

So when all the animals went to sleep, Coyote lay down too. But Coyote was only pretending to sleep. He was going to stay awake until the sunrise and then get the longest bow for himself.

But as the night went on, Coyote grew more and more sleepy. He got up and walked around, but still he was sleepy. He scratched at his eyes and started jumping and hopping about, but the sound woke up a few of the other animals. Coyote had to find another way to stay awake.

When the first star in the morning sky came up, still some time before the sun would rise, Coyote just could not keep his eyes open anymore. So he found two sticks and made them sharp and pointy. Then he stuck them in his eyelids. Now Coyote felt sure his eyes would stay open long enough for him to be the first one to meet the man and get the longest bow.

But in no time at all, Coyote was sound asleep. The pointy sticks had broken right through the skin of his eyelids and instead of keeping his eyes open, the sticks pinned Coyote's eyes shut. When all the other animals got up, Coyote did not stir from his deep sleep.

The longest bow went to Cougar, and to Bear the next longest. And so the bows were given until the last one for Frog.

But there was still one left over—the shortest bow. The man called out, "Which animal has not received a bow?" The animals all went to find out who was missing and they saw Coyote still sleeping on the ground. They laughed a great-hearted laugh and danced all around him.

The animals were laughing so hard that the man felt sorry for Coyote. Now Coyote would get the shortest bow and be the weakest one of them all. So the man prayed to Kareya for Coyote and Kareya made Coyote the cleverest and most tricky of the all the animals. And that's how Coyote got to be so tricky.

Bringing It Home

To Do This Week

❏ Why do you think Coyote believed the first one to meet the man would get the longest bow? If you were the man, would you do it that way?

❏ Draw or paint a picture of the longest bow and arrow.

❏ Tell a story about when you were given a special gift, award, or prize. Did you believe you deserved it?

❏ Why do you think Kareya chose the man to give the bows? Why didn't Kareya do it himself?

❏ Talk about what happens when you want something that everyone else in the family also wants.

❏ Imagine you are Coyote. At the end of the story, if you could do it all over again, what would you do differently?

Blessing for Meals of the Week

Let the corn come and
Let it not dry up but be full of kernels,
Ready for our pots and the cook-fire,
For now I am eating.

—TRADITIONAL NATIVE AMERICAN PRAYER

Prayer for the Week

You, Shamash, our God,
Climb to the highest mountains overlooking the earth.
You care for all the people in all the lands below.
Every creature, every person who breathes,
Is in the keeping of your hands.
The weak one calls out to you,
From the opening of the mouth.
The humble, the hurt, and the poor call out to you.
You, O God, give wisdom to see and
Make the difficult simple to understand.

—ADAPTED FROM A TRADITIONAL BABYLONIAN PRAYER

Week 35

Why Nahum Was Grateful
—TRADITIONAL JEWISH STORY

Sukhot, the harvest festival, was approaching. Nahum of Chernobyl wanted nothing more than to celebrate this holiday with the greatest of joy. And what really made the celebration joyous was having an etrog, a sacred citrus fruit, from the Holy Land.

But that year there had been a terrible drought in Israel and the fruits were very scarce. In all of Chernobyl only one person had been able to acquire an etrog—the richest man in town, Moshe Haim. Nahum was grief-stricken at the thought of not having an etrog for Sukhot, but what could he, a very poor man, give the wealthy Moshe Haim to obtain it?

Nahum possessed only one thing of real worth—the prayer shawl he had inherited from the holy rabbi, the Baal Shem Tov. Could Nahum let this sacred shawl go? On the other hand, could the Festival of Joy be truly celebrated without an etrog? Nahum made up his mind and raced to Moshe Haim's house. "I want to buy your etrog!" he proclaimed.

Moshe Haim laughed at him. "Where would a poor man like you ever get the money?"

Tenderly, Nahum held out the prayer shawl. "Would you take this in exchange?" he asked. "It once belonged to the Baal Shem Tov." Moshe Haim stood breathless before the Holy Master's prayer shawl.

"All right," he said finally. "You may have the etrog," and with that he took the shawl and placed the precious yellow fruit into Nahum's waiting hands.

Nahum was filled with joy. As if he had the wings of angels, Nahum flew home to show his wife the precious etrog.

"How did you pay for it?" she screamed at Nahum. "We don't even have money to buy enough food for the holiday!"

Nahum answered calmly, "I gave the Baal Shem Tov's prayer shawl in trade."

Nahum's wife flashed with anger. She grabbed the etrog from his hands and threw it to the ground. The top of the fruit broke off; now it couldn't be used for the holiday at all!

For a moment, Nahum became very angry, but then his face softened. In a gentle voice he said, "Yesterday we owned a treasure of treasures—the Holy Master's shawl. Today we possessed another great prize—a magnificent etrog. Now both are gone. But we still have each other, so let's stop fighting. Let's celebrate!"

Bringing It Home

To Do This Week

❏ Name one person in your family whom you are thankful for. Write that name down on a special piece of paper and keep it in a special place. Name one friend you are thankful for. Add that name to your special paper.

❏ Name one person in the world you really are grateful is alive now. Add that name to your paper.

❏ Write your own name on your special paper and at the top of the page write: "I am grateful for. . . ."

❏ Show each other your special gratitude papers, and talk about them.

Blessing for Meals of the Week

O Lord, the eyes of all wait upon you and
You give them their food in due season.
You open your hand and provide
All living beings with abundance.

—FROM A TRADITIONAL ARMENIAN PRAYER

Prayer for the Week

May the god who has become angry with me become calm toward me;
May the goddess who has become angry with me become calm
toward me.
Without knowing I have eaten that forbidden by my god;
I have set food on that forbidden by my goddess.
May your heart, like the heart of a real mother, become calm
toward me;
Like a real mother and a real father may you become calm
toward me.

—FROM A TRADITIONAL MESOPOTAMIAN PRAYER

The Home of Fools
—TRADITIONAL JEWISH STORY

Chelm was a little village in Poland known as the home of fools. In the village lived a shoemaker who one day headed for the big city of Warsaw. It was a long way to walk, and after a while the poor shoemaker grew very tired. But he was afraid to lie down and go to sleep. "Whichever way I look," he said to himself, "the road seems exactly the same. When I wake up, I won't know which way to go."

So the shoemaker thought up a clever idea. Before he lay down to sleep, he took off his boots. He placed one boot with the toe pointing toward the big city and the other one with the heel pointing back home to Chelm.

But as luck would have it, while the shoemaker snored away in a deep sleep, a forester's wagon passed by and a tree branch hanging over the side bumped into the shoemaker's boots. The boots got all turned around and now the toe of one boot pointed to Chelm, his hometown, and the heel of the other to Warsaw, the strange big city.

So what did the shoemaker do when he woke up and looked at his boots? What else? He followed the toe straight back to Chelm!

He walked right by the village marketplace with its few small shops. He passed the little synagogue where the people came to study and pray. "Why did people tell me so much about the wonderful things I'd see in Warsaw?" he wondered. "We have things just like this in Chelm."

Soon he saw a small stone house that looked exactly like his own, and in the house was a woman and six young girls who smiled happily at him. They were the very image of his own wife and six daughters. And when the woman and girls hugged and kissed him as if he was their husband and father returning home from a journey, the shoemaker thought, "I must have a twin here in Warsaw and this must be his home. I'll stay here and wait till he returns."

And anyone who has been to Chelm will tell you, that is where the shoemaker lived for the rest of his life!

Bringing It Home

To Do This Week

❑ Draw or paint a picture of the village of Chelm. Imagine you are the shoemaker. Draw or paint a picture of what the big city would have looked like to him if he had actually gotten there.

❑ Write down three things you really like about living in your home with your family. Write down three places you'd like to visit or live. Discuss what you wrote with your family.

❑ Tell a story about when someone in the family was away for a while and came back home.

❑ Imagine you've just come home after being away a long time. Draw or paint a picture that shows what happens.

Blessing for Meals of the Week

O Lord of the universe,
Please take all this good and bless it.
You gave this food to us,
For service to all,
Only you can bless it.

—ADAPTED FROM A TRADITIONAL HINDU PRAYER

Prayer for the Week

I speak to you, O God, Ahura Mazda.
With open arms and mind and my whole heart
I greet You in spirit.
My joy is in You,
My place of safety is in You,
My peace is in You.
Let me live before your eyes and
With You, O God.
This is my humble prayer.

—TRADITIONAL ZOROASTRIAN PRAYER

How Yima Saved Everyone From the Terrible Winter

—ADAPTED FROM A TRADITIONAL ZOROASTRIAN STORY

The coldest winter was about to come, a winter like none the world had ever seen before. This winter would destroy all the creatures of the earth if something was not done to save them.

So Ahura Mazda, the Creator, spoke to Yima, the first man and the first king of the earth, to tell him what was going to happen. "O Yima," he said, "upon all the living things in the world, both animals and plants, will fall a killing frost, and snow so heavy that the highest mountains will be covered.

"Before this terrible winter, the earth gave plenty of grass for cattle. Now the beasts that live in the wild places, from the mountaintops to the sweet meadows of the valleys, will have to find shelter under the earth. When the snow melts, O Yima, it will be a wonder to see the footprint of a sheep!

"O Yima," Ahura Mazda said, "this is what you must do. Make a place for the creatures to live and close it off on all sides so that they may be safe. Bring to that place oxen and sheep, human beings, dogs, birds, creatures of all kinds, and fires that burn red and hot.

"Build a special place, O Yima, for human beings to live and also one for the birds," Ahura Mazda told the man. "For the birds, make a stream flow in a pool. There the green plants will grow forever and the birds will always have food.

"You, too, shall build a house there, a big house, with a place from which to look out and a great yard in which to walk," Ahura Mazda said to Yima. "May all of you live a life of perfect happiness."

Bringing It Home

To Do This Week

❏ Pretend you are Yima. What would you say when Ahura Mazda told you this awful winter was coming?

❏ Draw or paint a picture of the world before the winter of destruction came. Draw or paint a picture of the world after the winter comes.

❏ Your family has a special assignment. Together, find out about some of the animals and plants that used to live on the earth but in the last fifty years have become extinct. Write down the names of ten of them. Find out about three animals or plants that almost became extinct but didn't because people did something to protect them. Talk about what those people did. Talk about what your family can do to keep all the living things of the earth alive.

Blessing for Meals of the Week

Blessed are You, O Lord our God,
King of the universe,
who feeds the whole world with
Your goodness, grace, kindness, and mercy.
You give food to all flesh,
for Your kindness endures forever.
Through Your great goodness,
we have never lacked food:
may it never fail us,
for the sake of Your great Name,
for You nourish and sustain all beings,
and do good to all,
and provide food for all Your creatures
whom You have created.
Blessed are You, O Lord,
who gives food to all.

—TRADITIONAL JEWISH BLESSING

Prayer for the Week

I sing for the animals,
Out of the earth I sing for them.
I sing for them.
Out of the earth
I sing for them,
The animals
I sing for them.

—TRADITIONAL NATIVE AMERICAN CHANT

Mulungu Leaves the Earth

—TRADITIONAL AFRICAN STORY

In the beginning there were no people on the earth. The good beasts lived peacefully with Mulungu, the Father of all creatures. One day Chameleon put a fish trap in the river and when he checked, it was full of fish. Chameleon took the fish home and ate them. So he put the trap in the river again, but when he pulled it out it was empty. "I have no luck today," he said. "I better set the trap again."

The next morning Chameleon found no fish in his trap. Instead there were two creatures he had never seen before—a little man and a little woman.

"What are they?" Chameleon wondered, and he took the creatures to Mulungu. "Father, look what I have brought!" Chameleon said.

Mulungu looked at the little man and woman and told Chameleon, "Take them out of the trap and put them on the earth. There they will grow."

Chameleon took them out and the little man and little woman grew on the earth. They grew until they were as tall as men and women are now.

The animals came to see what the man and woman would do. The man and the woman rubbed sticks together and made a fire. The fire jumped from bush to bush and swept through the whole forest. The animals had to run very fast to get away from the fire.

The man and the woman hunted a buffalo and killed the animal and cooked it on the fire. Then they ate it. The next day they killed an animal again, roasted it on the fire they made, and ate it. So they did every day.

Mulungu said, "They are burning everything all up with the fires they make! And they are killing all my animals!"

The beasts ran as far away from the man and woman as they could go. Chameleon ran up into the tall trees.

Mulungu said, "I'm leaving the earth!" He asked Spider, "How do you climb up so high?"

"Very well," said Spider to Mulungu, and Spider made a web-rope for Mulungu to climb.

Mulungu climbed the rope all the way into the sky and there he lives.

Bringing It Home

To Do This Week

❏ The fire the man and woman made ended up burning through the forest. Tell a story about when something you did caused a really big problem. Tell a story about something someone else did that caused a big problem—something you saw or knew about right after it happened.

❏ Imagine you were the man or the woman. What would you have done differently?

❏ Imagine you are Mulungu. When you saw what was happening on the earth, what would you do?

❏ Imagine you are Chameleon or one of the other animals at the end of the story. What would you say to the man and to the woman? What would you say to Mulungu?

Blessing for Meals of the Week

Great Spirit, may our thoughts
Reach out to the holy skies.
Give us good water and
Plenty of food.
Remember we are your children.

—ADAPTED FROM A TRADITIONAL NATIVE AMERICAN PRAYER

Prayer for the Week

We call upon the earth,
With all its beautiful deep places and
With all its high places
With all its living things and great life-spirit and
We ask the earth together to
Teach us and show us the way.

—TRADITIONAL NATIVE AMERICAN PRAYER

It All Started With . . .
—TRADITIONAL HINDU STORY

A man who wished to live a saintly life went to his teacher and said, "O guru, bringer of light into the darkness, how shall I become a saint, a true sadhu? Please tell me."

The guru told the man to own as little as possible and to live as simply as he could. So the student gave up his possessions and moved to a tiny shack far from other people. Every day, after his morning devotional rituals, he'd wash and hang out to dry his loincloth, the only thing he owned. One day he discovered birds had pecked holes in it, and since he had nothing else to wear, he went to the village to beg for a new one.

A few days later the new loincloth met an identical fate. "Well," the villagers said, "you not only need a loincloth, but you need a cat to protect it from the birds." So the man asked for and got a cat.

Then he needed to beg for milk to feed the cat. After a time the villagers grew weary of giving him milk for the cat. "You need to keep a cow," they told the poor man.

So he went and asked for a cow. Once he had the cow, he needed hay to feed the cow. His neighbors told him to stop begging and grow his own hay; there was plenty of farmland to be had.

So the simple man became a farmer. Soon he had to build barns and hire laborers. Now, because he was a landholder, he married, had children, and spent his days like all the other busy householders.

After a while, his guru came to visit the area and the now prosperous farm. Finding the farm filled with goods and buzzing with servants, the guru inquired of one, "A poor holy man used to dwell in these parts. Do you know where he has gone?" Receiving no answer, the guru went to the main house where he ran into his surprised student. "What happened?" the guru asked.

The man fell at the feet of his master and pitifully said, "My Lord, it all started with a single loincloth."

Bringing It Home

To Do This Week

❑ Draw or paint a picture of the simple holy man at the beginning of the story. Draw or paint a picture of the man at the end of the story when his guru came to visit.

❑ The man started with a cat and ended up with a very different kind of life than the one he wanted to have. Tell a story about how something you did turned out much different than you wanted.

❑ Tell a story about seeing that happen to someone else.

❑ Pretend you are the man. How could you have seen what would happen to you?

Blessing for Meals of the Week

Lord, you clothe the lilies,
you feed the birds of the sky,
you lead the lambs to pasture,
and the deer to the waterside,
you multiplied loaves and fishes,
and changed the water to wine;
come to our table as giver,
and as our guest to dine.

—TRADITIONAL CHRISTIAN SCOTTISH PRAYER

Prayer for the Week

Blessed by the Lord be this land
with the greatness of the ancient mountains,
with the abundance of the everlasting hills,
and with all the treasures of the earth in its perfection.

—FROM HEBREW SCRIPTURES

We Are All Related

— TRADITIONAL JEWISH STORY

King Solomon wanted to build a great temple for people to pray to God. He wanted to build on the holiest of places in all Israel, but what spot was that?

One night, it is said, Solomon took a long walk in the fields. He saw a man carrying heavy sacks of wheat, one after the other, from one barn to another barn nearby. Then the man slipped away into the dark night. "He must be a thief," Solomon thought, but he decided to keep watching.

Soon a different man appeared. He did the same thing, only he carried the sacks of wheat back to the original barn! Then he, too, left in silence.

The next day Solomon commanded the first man to see him. "Why do you steal wheat from your neighbor in the middle of the night?" he asked him.

The man replied, "No, I do not steal. My neighbor is my brother. He has a wife and many children to feed while I do not. He needs much more than I do, but he won't take any extra wheat from me. So every night I secretly carry wheat from my barn to his."

Then Solomon asked the other man to come and asked him why he took wheat from his barn and put it in another. The man answered, "I have the help of my whole family, but my brother has none. He has to pay for help, and so he needs more wheat. He won't take it from me, so in the night I secretly give the wheat to him."

Solomon brought the two men together and told them what each of them had done. "No wonder my pile of wheat sacks always stays the same," they both said, and laughed. And then they embraced each other with a hug full of love!

Solomon said, "Now I know the holiest place in all Israel! It is your land, where brothers love each other this much. So the temple shall be built here!"

Bringing It Home

To Do This Week

❏ Tell a story about how you did something in secret for someone or an animal. How did you feel? Tell a story about when someone did something for you in secret and then you found out who did it. How did you feel?

❏ Imagine you are King Solomon and you've just discovered what the two brothers had done for each other. What would you do?

❏ Draw or paint a picture of the great temple that was built on the two brothers' land.

❏ If you were a member of either of the two families and you knew that your family's wheat was being given away, what would you do?

❏ Tell a story about a person or animal (or anything else) that you feel is a part of your family.

Blessing for Meals of the Week

Earth who gives to us this food
Sun who makes it ripe and good
Dear Earth dear Sun
By you we live
Our loving thanks to you we give.

—BLESSING FROM REV. NICOLA AMADORA,
INTERFAITH MINISTER

Prayer for the Week

The perfume flowers are our sisters;
The deer, the horse, these are our brothers;
The rocky crest, the juices in the meadow,
The body heat of the pony and men
All belong to the same family.

—TEACHING OF NATIVE AMERICAN CHIEF SEATHL

The Golden Fish That Made Wishes Come True
—TRADITIONAL GERMAN FOLKTALE

Once upon a time there lived a very poor fisherman and his wife in a small cottage by the sea. Although the fisherman worked very hard, the couple had very little and his wife was never satisfied. She scolded him when he returned home having caught only a few fish.

One morning the fisherman threw his heavy nets into the sea hoping to catch a lot of fish. But there was only one, a bright golden fish!

The fisherman was amazed to see such a strange fish and he was even more amazed when the fish talked! "Please, kind fisherman," the golden fish said, "Let me go. If you let me go, I will make any wish of yours come true, for I am the son of the King of the Sea!"

The fisherman was so startled that he tossed the fish back into the sea without thinking about a wish at all. When he told his wife about the golden fish and the wish it had promised to fulfill, she was very angry.

"Go back," she yelled at him, "and ask for a new tub for washing. See how bad the old one looks? That is my wish!"

So the poor fisherman went back and called out to the golden fish, "Please come. My wife has a wish!" And the golden fish suddenly appeared and said, "It's good you have come. Now tell me what your wish is."

"My wife wants a new washtub," the fisherman said. And the golden fish said, "Go home. You will find it there just as I promised."

The fisherman's wife was very pleased at first with the wonderful new tub. But then she thought, "It is just a washtub. I should have asked for a big house!" She nagged her husband to go back and talk to the golden fish again.

At the shore he cried, "Golden fish, golden fish, please come again."

The golden fish popped its head out of the water and asked, "Are you here for another wish?"

"My wife wishes for a big house," the fisherman said softly.

"Very well," the golden fish said. "Since you were so kind to me and let me go, I'll grant you one more wish."

The fisherman was pleased to make his wife happy, but when he returned she stood in front of the big house and said, "Hurry back to that fish! We shouldn't be happy with a house like this when we can have a palace—and fancy clothes and jewels, too!"

The fisherman sadly went back and called on the golden fish to grant his wife's new wish. The golden fish agreed to make the palace and all the precious things too, but not so pleasantly as before. Still the fisherman was glad his wife was getting her demands satisfied.

How magnificent the palace was! The fisherman's wife stood all dressed up and covered with sparkling jewels. As the fisherman approached, she shouted at him, "Go back again!" But the fisherman stopped her.

"Can't we be satisfied with this? What more could we possibly need?"

"No!" she yelled. "Go ask the fish to make me a queen!"

This time the sky was black and stormy over the sea. Lightning flashed and the fisherman saw the golden fish swimming on the big waves. He told the golden fish his wife's wish. But the golden fish said nothing and then disappeared in the dark sea.

Another flash of lightning lit up the sky and the fisherman saw that the palace had disappeared. Everything the golden fish had given was gone and the old house stood right where it had always been.

The fisherman's wife cried and cried, but the fisherman did not shed a tear. In his heart he was content with what they had. The fisherman went fishing every day after that but never saw the golden fish again.

Bringing It Home

To Do This Week

- ❏ Draw or paint a picture of the golden fish.

- ❏ Make one wish. Talk about why you made that one wish.

- ❏ Talk about three things you've asked for and received. Were you happy with what you got or did you ask for more?

- ❏ Pretend you are the fisherman's wife at the end of the story. Do you want the golden fish to come back again?

Blessing for Meals of the Week

O, today we pray to
All that is holy
May we have enough to eat and
May everyone have enough to eat
This is our prayer today.

—FROM REV. AARON ZERAH

Prayer for the Week

I give beauty to all the earth
I am the breeze that refreshes all green things
I encourage blossoms to flourish with ripening fruits.
I am led by the spirit to feed the purest streams.
I am the rain coming from the dew
that causes the grasses to laugh with the joy of life.
I am the yearning for good.

—FROM HILDEGARD OF BINGEN

Stones on the Road

—TRADITIONAL JEWISH STORY

A very, very rich man lived in a very, very large house. His servants made a lovely garden for him, so that even in the hottest days of summer the rich man could sit in the cool shade of his tall trees.

Still, the rich man was always thinking about more things his servants could do for him. He commanded them to dig new gardens and build more stone walls around his property.

When the servants dug through the earth, they found many rocks, far too many for them to use. They went to the rich man and asked, "Master, what should we do with all these extra stones?"

The rich man pointed to a wall and said, "Just throw them over that wall into the road." And because the master ordered them to do it, the servants tossed the stones into the road where everybody walked. They did this day after day.

At last, a wise old man came walking along and saw the stones being tossed into the road. He asked the servants why they were throwing stones onto the road and they said, "Our master told us to."

So the wise old man went to see their master, the rich man, and asked, "Why are you throwing stones from what belongs to you to what does not belong to you?"

The rich man paid little attention to the old man. "All I care about," the rich man said, "is that I get these stones off my property."

"But what about all the people who must walk on this road?" the old man asked.

The rich man said, "Why should I care about them?" and started to walk away.

The wise old man said to himself, "I believe someday you will wish you had not said what you have said." And the wise old man left.

After that day, everything went badly for the rich man. All the things that used to make money for him now failed, and he lost all that he owned. The rich man was forced to leave his big house and walk the very road on which he had ordered his servants to throw stones. The same stones badly hurt his feet and the rich man thought, "The wise old man was right to ask about throwing stones from what belonged to me to what did not belong to me. How I wish that I had cared then!"

Bringing It Home

To Do This Week

❏ Draw or paint a picture of the rich man's garden.

❏ Imagine you are a servant of the rich man. When he tells you to dig out more rocks all day long, how do you feel about him?

❏ Tell a story about when you cared only about yourself and didn't think about what would happen to others because of what you did. Tell a story about when someone else didn't seem to care about you and just did what they wanted to do.

❏ Imagine you are the wise old man. When the rich man didn't listen to you, what would you do?

❏ Imagine you see the rich man, now very poor, walking down the road with no shoes and bruised feet. What would you do?

Blessing for Meals of the Week

May the blessing of God
Rest upon all who are kind to us
Care for us, work for us, serve us and
Share at this table our bread.

—ADAPTED FROM CHRISTIAN COPTIC EGYPTIAN PRAYER

Prayer for the Week

Every day the sun rises
Each person must move every joint in the body
To do kind-hearted acts
A good word is such an act
Each step you take to pray is a kind-hearted act, and
Removing a dangerous thing from a road is, as well,
A kind-hearted act.

—ADAPTED FROM A TRADITIONAL MUSLIM TEACHING

When Daniel Faced the Hungry Lions

—TRADITIONAL STORY FROM HEBREW SCRIPTURES

Daniel was thrown into a dark hole in the ground. There were lions all around, ready to tear him to pieces. He heard their growling and roaring and they sounded hungry.

"O God," Daniel prayed, "help me! Keep me from the mouths of these lions!"

Daniel's friend, King Darius of Babylon, waited to see what would happen to him. He hoped Daniel would come out alive.

Daniel's enemies were happy. They had tricked King Darius into punishing Daniel and now they were sure Daniel would be killed.

They were jealous of Daniel because he was the king's most trusted advisor and friend. They believed King Darius didn't think they were so important anymore.

So the wicked advisors came up with a plan. They went to the palace and bowed before the king. "O Great One," they said to him, "everyone knows all good things are gifts from you."

The king was delighted to hear this. "Go on," he told them.

"As this is true," the men said, "then no one should be permitted to pray to anyone but you, King Darius." Again they bowed.

"You're right," said the king. "I am greater than any of the gods."

So the king made a law that no one in the kingdom could pray to anyone but him and disobeying the law meant death. That's how the advisors fooled the king. They knew when they praised him as the greatest god he would forget that Daniel prayed to the living God, not the king, and that Daniel always would.

Daniel prayed to God three times every day and when he heard the new law he still prayed to God. The advisors told the king and he was forced to give Daniel to the lions. He couldn't let Daniel go and punish others for doing the same thing.

The sun came up. And now the king and all the advisors could see what happened to Daniel. He was alive! He cried out, "My God sent an angel to protect me. Look, the lions are asleep and did not hurt me!"

King Darius commanded that the wicked advisors be thrown in with the lions and told everyone in the kingdom, "Daniel's God is the living God who does the greatest of things."

Bringing It Home

To Do This Week

❏ Draw or paint a picture of the lions Daniel faced.

❏ Tell a story about when you were in great trouble, like Daniel was with the lions roaring all around him.

❏ The first thing Daniel did in the pit was get very still and quiet. How do you think he felt before he got still? How do you think he felt after?

❏ Is there a word or name that you call the one to whom you speak in prayer? Say that name silently.

❏ Join all your hands together, and silently pray, like Daniel did, three times.

❏ Today when you see a stranger who looks troubled, make a prayer for her or him.

Blessing for Meals of the Week

Let the people praise you, O God:
Let all people praise you.
Then shall the earth bring forth her increase and
God, even our own God, shall bless us and
All the ends of the world shall
Look upon God with awe.

—TRADITIONAL PRAYER FROM HEBREW SCRIPTURES

Prayer for the Week

Wherever I go, only You!
Wherever I stand, only You!
Only You, again You
Always You!

—ADAPTED FROM A TRADITIONAL CHASSIDIC JEWISH SONG

Week 44

On the Way to the Promised Land
—TRADITIONAL STORY FROM HEBREW SCRIPTURES

Moses, Aaron, and their sister Miriam led the Hebrews out of slavery in Egypt and into the desert wilderness. They believe that God was taking them to the land where they would be free and happy, the land God had promised them.

God had provided water for them where no water appeared to be—it came out of a rock! And God had given them food—the miraculous manna that arose like dew around the bushes every day. There was always enough manna for everyone and it tasted good, too!

When the people were near the promised land, Moses sent his young helper Joshua, along with Joshua's friend Caleb and ten other spies, to see

what the land of Canaan was like. The people could hardly wait for the twelve men to return!

The spies brought back a very happy surprise with them. "Look at the fruit that grows in the rich country!" they shouted. "The grapes are so heavy two of us had to carry the bunches together!"

The Hebrews were very glad to hear the good news. They were ready to go!

But ten of the spies looked sad and said, "The cities have great walls around them and the people there are like giants compared to us!"

Then the Hebrews let out an awful cry. "Why did we come to this place?" they complained, "We can never go into this land and live there!"

Joshua and Caleb then spoke up. "God promised us that we would live in a good land. Let's go!"

But the people listened to the ten discouraged spies and not to Joshua and Caleb. "We'll all be killed!" they shouted at Moses, "Let's give up and go back to Egypt!"

God heard the cries of the Hebrews and said to Moses, "These people do not believe that the land I promised them is theirs. They will not go in, but wander in this desert for many years. Their children will go into the land I promised and Joshua and Caleb, too, for they believed."

Bringing It Home

To Do This Week

❏ Draw or paint a picture of the delicious fruit the spies brought back with them. Draw or paint a picture of the gigantic people and strong walled cities the ten spies told everyone about.

❏ Tell a story about when you were afraid to do something you really wanted to do and you gave up. How did you feel? Tell a story about when you were afraid to do something you really wanted to do and you did it anyway. How did you feel?

❏ Talk about what makes you believe you can do something even when the people around you don't think it can be done.

❏ Draw or paint a picture of the grown-up children, and Joshua and Caleb, when they finally arrived in the promised land.

Blessing for Meals of the Week

From the heavens you send water to fall on the hills, and
The earth is rich with your blessings.
You make the grass grow for the cattle to eat and
Green plants for all the people.
From the earth people bring forth wine to gladden the heart,
Oil to make us shine, and
Bread to give us strength.

—TRADITIONAL PRAYER FROM HEBREW SCRIPTURES

Prayer for the Week

Make this prayer at sunset and the beginning of the day:
O Lord make me to enter
In a good way the places I go, and
Make me go out from those places
In a good way.
Give me your helping power.

—ADAPTED FROM PRAYER IN THE QUR'AN, HOLY BOOK OF ISLAM

Lord Krishna and the Two Men

—TRADITIONAL HINDU STORY

It is told in India that Lord Krishna wished to see if the kings of his land were wise. So he called first a king named Duryodana.

Duryodana was known as a cruel man and the people in his kingdom feared him. Lord Krishna told Duryodana that he was to take a journey throughout the lands. "I want you," Lord Krishna said, "to look for one truly good person for me."

Duryodana obeyed Lord Krishna and began his travels. He found many different kinds of people and spoke to them about many things. After a long time away, Duryodana returned to Lord Krishna and said, "Lord, I have done what you commanded me and looked the whole world over for one truly good soul. Such a person I could not find. Each one I met was selfish and evil-minded. A truly good person cannot be found anywhere!"

Lord Krishna sent Duryodana on his way and called King Dhammaraja to see him. Dhammaraja was known as a kind man who tried to help people in his kingdom, who loved him very much. Lord Krishna said to King Dhammaraja, "I want you to journey throughout all the lands and find me one truly evil person."

Dhammaraja said, "As you wish, my Lord," and like Duryodana he set off on a long journey.

After much time had passed, Dhammaraja came to Lord Krishna and said, "My Lord, I have not brought back the one truly evil person you wished to see. I found that people make mistakes; I found that they are fooled by others; I found that they act as if they are blind. But I could not find a truly evil person. The people all are good in their hearts!"

Bringing It Home

To Do This Week

❑ When you are going to meet a group of new people, what do you think? How do you feel?

❑ Tell a story about when someone new moved into your neighborhood or first came to your school or workplace.

❑ Tell someone in your family about how you thought there was something bad about her or him that now you see differently.

❑ Imagine you are King Duryodana. When you went back to your kingdom, what would you do?

❑ Today shake the hand of each person in your family and say, "You are a good person. Thank you for being my friend."

Blessing for Meals of the Week

Around our table,
May all who share the
Delights of this season
Enjoy countless more.

—TRADITIONAL CHINESE BLESSING

Prayer for the Week

Father, I am here before you.
All people are good in my eyes.
God, it is you
Who judges the differences
Between us people.

—TRADITIONAL AFRICAN PRAYER

Who Is the Oldest?

—TRADITIONAL BUDDHIST STORY

A long time ago a monkey, an elephant, and a partridge lived as neighbors in the Himalayan Mountains. They were friends of a sort but often were rude and disrespectful to each other.

One day they met under a great banyan tree and said, "Let's decide to treat the oldest one of us with real respect. That will be a better way to live." And the three agreed.

But which one of them was the oldest? The monkey, the elephant, and the partridge thought about this question and at last discovered a way to find out.

"My dear elephant," the other two said, "we all sit under this same banyan tree. How tall was it when you first saw it?"

"Good friends," the elephant answered, "when I was very small, I walked right over this tree. And when I stood upon it, the highest branches of the tree that now seem to touch the sky tickled my belly. You see, I am so old that I knew the tree as just a little bush."

Then the elephant and the partridge asked the monkey and he said, "Good friends, when I was little more than a baby, I used to sit and reach up my head to eat the green shoots at the very top of the banyan. Since it began growing, I have known the tree."

The monkey and the elephant now turned to the partridge to ask how long he had known the tree. "Good friends," the partridge said, "there grew near this spot a great banyan tree very much like the one under which we are now sitting. I used to fly up into that great banyan and eat of its fruit, and drop its seeds all around. That is how this banyan tree came to grow here. So I knew this banyan even before it was born. That makes me the oldest!"

The monkey and the elephant bowed in respect to the clever partridge. "You are the oldest of us in wisdom," they said, "and we will listen to you and follow your teaching."

From that time on the monkey, the elephant, and the partridge were polite and respectful to each other. They all did what was right and lived a holy and happy life together.

Bringing It Home

To Do This Week

❏ This week have the youngest one in the family lead the blessing and the oldest one in the family lead the prayer.

❏ Think about your parents, uncles and aunts, and grandparents. How are you like them?

❏ Tell a story about when someone older than you helped you to do something you weren't sure how to do yourself. Tell a story about when you showed someone younger than you how to do something.

❏ Is there something you know how to do better than your parents or your elders? Talk about how you can teach them.

❏ Imagine you could visit with anyone who ever lived on the earth. When you meet, what would you ask?

Blessing for Meals of the Week

Blessed are you, Lord.
You have fed us from our earliest days,
You give food to all living creatures,
Fill our hearts with joy and delight.

—ANCIENT CHRISTIAN PRAYER

Prayer for the Week

O my guardians, from most ancient time,
Watch over our home
From top to bottom,
From one corner to the other,
From east to west,
From the side where we see the land,
To the side where we view the sea.
From the inside to the outside,
Watch over and protect our home.
Keep away all that may trouble our life,
Anana—our prayer is released.

—TRADITIONAL HAWAIIAN PRAYER

Week 47

They Made a Lion

—TRADITIONAL HINDU STORY

In India long ago lived four friends. Because of the families in which they were born, they were supposed to study all the holy books and become Brahmins, leaders of the people and advisors to kings.

Three of them read books all day long and knew as much as any learned scholar. But they knew little about real life. The fourth didn't want to study much; he went out exploring and developed a great deal of sense.

One day the four men met and said, "Let us travel to see the king. We shall find favor with him and become rich. Since we are friends, we'll share our wealth!"

But on the way, the first Brahmin thought, "The king gives riches only to great scholars, not to people who only have sense. Only the three of us who are scholars should have a share."

The three Brahmins argued for a while, but finally agreed that the fourth Brahmin, stupid as he seemed to them, could come along. So all four kept on their way through the forest path.

Soon the four friends came upon the dried up bones of a dead lion. "With our great knowledge," the three scholars thought, "we can bring this creature back to life!"

The first Brahmin said, "I know how to put all the bones back in the right order."

The second one said, "I can make the flesh and blood, and cover the beast with skin, too!"

The third one said, "I can give it breath and make it live again!"

So the first Brahmin got the skeleton together and the second one the flesh and blood and skin. The third Brahmin was just about to give the breath of life when the fourth, the only one who had sense, cried out, "Don't you know that is a lion? If you bring the beast back to life, it will kill us all!"

"You have not studied like we have!" the three Brahmins said. "We won't let you stop us!"

"If you won't listen to my sensible advice," the fourth one said, "I'm going to climb this tree."

The fourth Brahmin looked down from his safe spot high up on a tree branch at the three scholars. The lion was brought back to life, got up on its legs, saw the three Brahmins—and instantly killed them all.

Bringing It Home

To Do This Week

❏ Draw or paint a picture of the dead lion's bones. Talk about why you think the three Brahmins wanted to make the lion live again.

❏ Tell a story about something you learned from a book that really helped you.

❏ Talk about one thing you really want to learn how to do. Today, take a step to learn to do that one thing. First, try doing it yourself.

❏ Sit still and take five deep breaths, in and out. Pay attention to where you sense the breaths in your body and then share your experience.

Blessing for Meals of the Week

O wonderful, O wonderful, O wonderful.
I am food, I am food, I am food.
I am an eater of food,
I am an eater of food,
I am an eater of food.

—TRADITIONAL HINDU PRAYER

Prayer for the Week

O God, Creator,
The One who is good to us,
Good day to you, God,
Good day.
I am learning, God;
Let me learn well.

—ADAPTED FROM A TRADITIONAL AFRICAN DRUM SONG

The Right Thing to Do

—TRADITIONAL ZEN BUDDHIST STORIES

In Japan, many families thought it was a great honor to have a child accept-ed as a student by a master teacher. When one went to become a holy monk, good behavior and self-discipline were expected.

Many stories were told about the great masters and how they taught the students in their care. Here are two of those stories.

The master Sengai had a student who would not stay in the temple rooms at night and be quiet like all the other boys. Rather, he would get up and climb over the walls and go to the near-by town to have fun.

One night Master Sengai looked in on the sleeping boys and found that the student was missing. He saw a very tall stool had been placed up against the wall. The boy had most certainly used the stool to escape over the wall and, when he returned, would surely step on it again to get back down on the floor.

Master Sengai moved the stool to the side. He then stood there in its place and waited.

* * *

Master Soyen Shaku was known as one who never wasted a moment. Though he was a tough taskmaster, especially on himself, he allowed his students to sleep on hot summer days.

When Master Soyen Shaku was but a boy of twelve, he was already studying very deep questions about what was right to do in life. He talked to the older monks as if he were a monk himself.

One summer day, while his teacher was away, Soyen became so sleepy in the stuffy air that he just lay down near the doorway and napped. Three hours later, little Soyen suddenly woke up. His master had come back!

But it was too late to move. There he was on the floor and the master was opening the door.

"I beg your pardon," Soyen's master said, as he most carefully stepped over his little student's body. "I beg your pardon."

Soyen never slept in the afternoon again.

Bringing It Home

To Do This Week

❑ Imagine you are the monk, Master Sengai. What would you do when you knew the boy was missing? Imagine you are the boy who escaped over the wall. When you came back and stepped on Master Sengai instead of the stool, what would you do?

❑ Pretend you are one of Master Sengai's other students and you know the boy is going to town to have fun. What would you do?

❑ Imagine you are the young Soyen Shaku. When you hear your teacher at the door, what would you do?

❑ Pretend you are Soyen Shaku's teacher and you see him lying sleepy-eyed on the floor. What would you do?

Blessing for Meals of the Week

We call on the land
Which grows food for us.
We call on the good earth and
The gardens of plenty.
We call on you
To show us the good way.

—FROM A TRADITIONAL NATIVE AMERICAN PRAYER

Prayer for the Week

May the road rise to meet you,
may the wind be always at your back,
may the sun shine warm on your face,
the rain fall softly on your fields;
and until we meet again,
may God hold you in the palm of his hand.

—TRADITIONAL IRISH BLESSING

Week 49

Who Am I?

Nasreddin brought a bow and arrows with him to the country fair. His students all came to see Nasreddin compete in the archery contest.

Like all other contestants, Nasreddin was given three shots at the target. Before he took his first shot, Nasreddin put on the kind of hat a soldier wears and stood up very straight. Then he pulled the bow back hard and fired. The arrow sailed over the target. Nasreddin missed the target completely, and everyone in the crowd laughed at him.

Nasreddin picked up the bow once more and drew it back. This time he used much less strength, and although the arrow flew straight at the target, it fell far short of it.

Nasreddin only had his third shot left. He simply turned to face the target and fired the third arrow. It hit dead center!

For a moment everyone in the whole crowd went crazy! Then, so surprised were they that the man they had laughed at had made a perfect last shot, they became totally silent.

Nasreddin made no fuss at all. He went over to get his prize for winning the contest and started walking away. But Nasreddin's students and everyone else wanted to know how he made the last shot after not even having come close with the first two.

"I'll tell you," Nasreddin said. "For the first shot I was imagining I was a soldier and a terrible enemy faced me. Fear caused the arrow to fly high over the target. When I took the second shot I was thinking like a man who had missed the first one and was so nervous he could not concentrate. He was weak with worry, and the shot was too."

Nasreddin paused. Finally a courageous soul spoke up. "And what about the third one? Who fired that arrow?"

"Oh," said Nasreddin. "That was me!"

—TRADITIONAL SUFI STORY
* * *

Who Am I?

Once upon a time in China there lived a man called Chuang-tzu. Chuang-tzu, like many others of his day, wished to know what was real and what was not.

Chuang-tzu had a dream and when he woke up this is what he said: "I, Chuang-tzu, dreamed that I was a butterfly, flying here and there. I thought only of things a butterfly takes a fancy to and thought about none of the things a man like myself does.

"Suddenly I woke up. There I was, Chuang-tzu, the man once more. Now I do not know if I am a man dreaming I was a butterfly or if I am a butterfly dreaming I am a man!"

—TRADITIONAL CHINESE TAOIST STORY

Bringing It Home

To Do This Week

❑ Draw a big circle on a special piece of paper. Make seven sections in the circle so it looks like this:

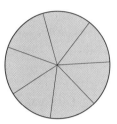

❑ You are going to complete a holy work of art—a mandala. In each of five of the sections, write or draw something you feel is true about yourself. Feel free to use different colors, different symbols, different designs and words. Write or draw as big or as small as you want.

❑ Think about one thing that is only true about you and no one else. Write or draw that in the sixth section.

❑ Is there someone you dream to be? In the last section describe or draw your dream. You have now completed your very own mandala. Share your mandala with the family.

Blessing for Meals of the Week

May the wind blow with sweetness;
May the waters flow with sweetness;
May the plants grow with sweetness;
For all people who are true.

—TRADITIONAL HINDU BLESSING

Prayer for the Week

I make footprints,
I stand among the wind-blown leaves;
I make footprints,
I stand with pride;
I make footprints,
I stand in a happy day.

—ADAPTED FROM A TRADITIONAL NATIVE AMERICAN SONG

Week 50

The Crow, the Fox, and the Cheese

—Greek fable of Aesop

A crow stole a piece of cheese one day and flew to the highest branches of a tree to sit and eat it. The crow had just taken the delicious treat in its beak and was about to swallow it when a clever fox sitting below called out, "O most wonderful bird, most glorious crow! How lucky I am to see your beauty today!" The crow listened to the words of the fox and smiled. But the cheese stayed gripped in the crow's beak and again she went to eat it.

The fox's mouth started to water. He shouted up at the crow, "You are truly the loveliest of all birds and although I have yet to hear your song, I am certain that you have the loveliest of voices, far sweeter than any other."

The crow was very pleased to hear the fox praise her so, especially the things he said about her voice. Why, no one else wanted to hear the crow sing. Everyone said her voice made their ears hurt!

The crow was delighted that the fox wished to hear her lovely song. She opened her beak to sing, and out popped the delicious cheese! It fell out of the crow's beak right into the fox's mouth.

That's how the crow lost her cheese and the clever fox got to eat it all.

Bringing It Home

To Do This Week

❏ Draw or paint a picture of the crow with the piece of cheese in her beak. Draw or paint a picture of the fox with his mouth watering.

❏ Tell a story about how you listened to somebody even though you knew they were lying. What happened? Tell a story about when you didn't tell the whole truth so you could get something you wanted. How did you feel?

❏ Imagine you are the crow. At the end of the story, how do you feel?

❏ Imagine you are the fox. At the end of the story, what do you think the crow will do next?

❏ Talk about one thing for which you love being praised. Share why this is so.

Blessing for Meals of the Week

All living beings are struggling for life,
May they all have enough food today.

—SPOKEN BY THICH NHAT HANH, BUDDHIST MONK

Prayer for the Week

Listen, O my people, and I will speak.
I am God, your God.
Every beast of the forest is mine, and
The cattle upon a thousand hills.
I know all the birds of the mountains, and
All the wild animals in the fields are mine.
Give thanks unto God and
Keep your promises to the One Most High.

— FROM HEBREW SCRIPTURES

How the Children Became Stars
—TRADITIONAL NATIVE AMERICAN STORY

Once, it is told, twelve children came together to play near the lodge-houses of their parents. They knew all sorts of games, but today they made up a new one. This is the game they played.

All the children joined hands and made a circle. They stood on the grass and each danced and sang, "We are dancing. We are dancing."

The parents listened to the children's song and watched the children dance. The children kept singing, "We are dancing. We are dancing." Then the parents saw something amazing. The children's feet no longer danced on the earth, but above it. The children were moving towards the sky.

The parents were very afraid and they ran to make the children stop their singing and dancing. But the children still danced and sang and soon they were high above their parents' reach and disappearing into the sky. The children sang, "We are dancing. We are dancing."

Higher and higher the children rose up into the sky, all the while holding hands, until they could no longer be seen at all.

Everyone kept looking out for the children and listening for their song, "We are dancing. We are dancing." At last they were seen. The children were the twelve stars that shone in the heavens above the lodge-houses of their parents. They were a circle of twelve stars with just one star a little bit out of place.

Every night when we look in the sky, we see these twelve stars and remember the twelve children who sang, "We are dancing. We are dancing."

Bringing It Home

To Do This Week

❑ Greet the sun and say, "Great Star, thank you for your light and warmth." At night go out and see the stars.

❑ Imagine you are one of the children and your feet started lifting off the ground. What would you do? Imagine you are one of the parents and you saw the children going into the sky. What would you do?

❑ Talk about or show your family something that makes you very, very happy.

❑ Notice all the things that you were happy about today. Write down the three you were most happy about.

❑ Imagine yourself as a star. Draw or paint a picture of yourself.

❑ Play some music that pleases the whole family—music you're all happy to listen to. Join hands in a circle and dance as the spirit moves you. Remember, you are all stars.

Blessing for Meals of the Week

May we become as stars
For everything is made of stars
May we become as stars
For all we eat is made of stars
May we become as stars
And brighten this day
The holy stars have given us.

—FROM REV. AARON ZERAH

Prayer for the Week

Grandfather, Great Spirit, you have been always,
and before you nothing has been.
There is no one to pray to but you.
The star nations all over the heavens are yours,
and yours are the grasses of the earth.
Grandfather, Great Spirit, fill us with the light.
Teach us to walk the soft earth as relatives to all that live.
Help us, for without you we are nothing.

—TRADITIONAL NATIVE AMERICAN PRAYER

Week 52

Crossing Over

—TRADITIONAL JEWISH STORY

When the slaves left Egypt and marched into an unknown desert, they hoped they would find a better life in a new land. In the great crowd were people from many different countries. Out of hunger, their ancestors had crossed over to Egypt long ago only to become trapped in servitude. Now at last they were free to go!

In the desert it was hard to know which way to go, but a great moving cloud came every day before the people and at night a great moving fire showed them the way. They soon came to a watery place called the Sea of Reeds. They had not seen an Egyptian for many, many days and once they passed over the sea they would be safe. A new life was possible!

But the people who were camping on the shore heard a terrible sound in the distance. It was the Egyptian army! They were coming fast with thousands of soldiers and hundreds of chariots! The horses' hooves pounded the sand as they ran toward the terrified people. The people looked to Moses for he was the one who had always dealt with Pharaoh before. Now Pharaoh and his awful army were upon them. They had no place to go but the sea!

Some wept bitter tears. "O, why did we ever leave Egypt?" they cried. Moses heard the word of God, the Holy One who said "I am always," and turned to the people.

"Be still in your hearts," he said, "and you shall see the Holy One will bring you across to safety. The Holy One says to you, 'Go forward!'"

Moses raised his rod high above the sea and reached out his hands. A strong wind from the east blew over the sea and began pushing the water to both sides.

As one of the people on the shore stepped into the sea, the earth appeared! A clear pathway opened and everyone started to cross over.

When the Egyptians saw the people who had been their slaves crossing over, they were amazed. The Egyptians whipped their horses and ran madly after the people to catch them before they reached the other side. But the chariots got stuck in the muddy earth and the Egyptian soldiers could not cross.

When the people had all crossed over, the wind stopped blowing and the waters of the sea crashed over the Egyptians.

From the first to the last, the people all had gone forward as the Holy One had told them. They had crossed over to freedom!

Bringing It Home

To Do This Week

❑ Imagine you are one of the people who chose to leave Egypt. When you first heard and saw the Egyptian army, what would you do?

❑ Draw or paint a picture of the Egyptian army with their horses and chariots. Now draw or paint the people camped out on the shore of the Sea of Reeds.

❑ Some of the people thought they were trapped between the Egyptian soldiers and the sea and could not cross over. Talk about times in your life you thought the same way.

❑ Imagine you are one of the Egyptians. When you saw the first person step into the sea, what did you think? Talk about what you think the people will find on the other side of the sea.

❑ Imagine you are one of the people who have crossed over. The clouds and the fire are no longer before you. How will you find your way?

❑ Light a candle, a holy flame, and let the whole family gather around it. All of you be still and breathe deep within. Then together say: "We call upon the Holy One to be with us now and always."

Blessing for Meals of the Week

O, Holy One
May we take the step
To be fed by you.
O Holy One
May we take the step
To feed everyone
On this good earth.

—FROM REV. AARON ZERAH

Prayer for the Week

O, Holy One,
Thank you, thank you, thank you.

—FROM REV. AARON ZERAH

Story Illustration Acknowledgments

BOOTH TARKINGTON ELEMENTARY SCHOOL, SOUTH BEND, IN
Patty Tokars, Art Teacher

Andrew Bradburn, 4th grade	Week 33, page 102
Matt Walker, 4th grade	Week 24, page 79
Travis Chapman, 5th grade	Week 37, page 114
Lisa Huang, 6th grade	Week 2, page 14

CHRISTIAN CENTER SCHOOL, SOUTH BEND, IN
Terry Nix, Art Teacher

Jordann Penrod, 4th grade	Week 15, page 56
Amber Sumrall, 5th grade	Week 12, page 47
Amy Larson, 6th grade	Week 44, page 132

DARDEN ELEMENTARY SCHOOL, SOUTH BEND, IN
Bonnie Brueseke, Art Teacher

Edsys Acuña, 5th grade	Week 41, page 123

MADISON ELEMENTARY SCHOOL, WAKARUSA, IN
Carissa Truex, Art Teacher

Nichole Hall, 4th grade	Week 23, page 76

MEADOW'S EDGE ELEMENTARY SCHOOL, MISHAWAKA, IN
Carissa Truex, Art Teacher

Holly Tavares, 4th grade	Week 3, page 18

QUEEN OF ALL SAINTS SCHOOL, MICHIGAN CITY, IN
Alison S. Jaksa, Art Teacher

Adam Donaldson, 4th grade	Week 36, page 111
Devan Pritz, 4th grade	Week 29, page 92
Joe Gushrowski, 5th grade	Week 6, page 28
Ashley Nowak, 6th grade	Week 51, page 151
Justin Milcarek, 6th grade	Week 48, page 143

SAINT ADALBERT CATHOLIC SCHOOL, SOUTH BEND, IN
Kristin Bentley, Art Teacher

Jessica Vaughn, 4th grade	Week 27, page 87
Jessica Hay, 5th grade	Week 20, page 69
Gerard M. Newhouse Jr., 6th grade	Week 43, page 129

SAINT BAVO SCHOOL, MISHAWAKA, IN
Jennifer Hendrix, Art Teacher
    Irene Robinson, 4th grade   Week 32, page 99
    Adam Langenbrunner, 5th grade   Week 46, page 137
    Jerome Krakowski, 6th grade   Week 25, page 82

SAINT JOSEPH GRADE SCHOOL, SOUTH BEND, IN
Jennifer Wheet, Art Teacher
    Christina Hegel, 5th grade   Week 30, page 94
    Chris Miller, 5th grade   Week 18, page 63
    Mary Brigid Halloran, 6th grade   Week 11, page 43
    Claire Fallon, 6th grade   Week 5, page 24

SAINT MATTHEW CATHEDRAL SCHOOL, SOUTH BEND, IN
Pat Varner, Art Teacher
    Brittany Sinka, 4th grade   Week 34, page 105
    Kirsten Brammer, 5th grade   Week 8, page 35
    Patrick Ranschaert, 6th grade   Week 52, page 154

WILSON ELEMENTARY SCHOOL, CINCINNATI, OH
Carey Bower, Art Teacher
    Drew Reynolds, 4th grade   Week 1, page 11
    Alex Byrd, 5th grade   Week 14, page 53
    Caitlin Hanna, 6th grade   Week 42, page 126

Special thanks to Pat Varner at St. Matthew Cathedral School and Carey Bower at Wilson Elementary School for their invaluable help getting this project off to a great start.

A note from the author.

I wish to add my acknowledgment—and blessings—to all the children whose works of art grace this book and make it far richer and more beautiful. To their teachers—and to all the great spiritual teachers and storytellers, both ancient and modern, whose wisdom is found within these pages, I say thank you. This book is a gift and I am honored to pass it on.

Today there is a great, diverse circle connecting people of faith from around the world who are moved to share their own stories, prayers, and blessings of all kinds. To connect with this circle, please contact

Spirit of Interfaith
136 Swift St.
Santa Cruz, CA 95060
www.spiritofinterfaith.org.

Aaron Zerah, a leading minister of the interfaith religious movement, embraces all traditions and peoples. As chancellor of Interfaith Seminaries and president of Spirit of Interfaith, Inc., he ministers to families, communities, and organizations throughout the world. The son of Holocaust survivors, he places special value on playing, singing, and dancing—living each day to the fullest. His previous book, *The Soul's Almanac: A Year of Interfaith Stories, Prayers and Wisdom*, is a collection of parables and quotes selected from all the world's faiths, illustrating the wisdom  revealed in the practices and writings of various cultures and religious traditions. Zerah lives in Northern California with his wife, Madhuri, and their daughter, Sari.